W9-BRV-405

"I found her like that. Just... just lying there...lifeless."

"I know." Bubba's voice cracked as emotion clogged his throat. "I need you to come to the living room now. Just a couple of questions." Duty called, despite his tangled emotions. "When did you talk to Tanty?"

Tara blinked. "Around ten-ish. I'd called to ask her a question."

"And why'd you come here tonight?"

"I've been training under Tanty."

Right. He remembered now. His aunt had stepped in as a role model for the youngest LeBlanc. "What time did you arrive?"

"About nine or so. When I didn't find her in the workhouse, I came here to look for her."

He glanced over the room. No sign of a struggle, no forced entry.

"Someone did this to her."

He jerked his attention back to Tara. "What?"

She met his stare dead-on. "She didn't just fall ill. Someone set out to hurt her."

Books by Robin Caroll

Love Inspired Suspense

Bayou Justice #74
Bayou Corruption #89
Bayou Judgment #101
Bayou Paradox #103

ROBIN CAROLL

Born and raised in Louisiana, Robin Caroll is a Southern belle right down to her "hey y'all." Her passion has always been to tell stories to entertain others. Robin's mother, bless her heart, is a genealogist who instilled in Robin the deep love of family and pride of heritage—two aspects Robin weaves into each of her books. When she isn't writing, Robin spends time with her husband of eighteen years, her three beautiful daughters, and their four character-filled cats at home—in the South, where else? An avid reader herself, Robin loves hearing from and chatting with other readers. Although her favorite genre to read is mystery/suspense, of course, she'll read just about any good story. Except historicals! To learn more about this author of deep-South mysteries of suspense to inspire your heart, visit Robin's Web site at www.robincaroll.com.

ROBIN CAROLL

BAYOU PARADOX

Steeple
Hill®

Published by Steeple Hill Books™

If you purchased this book without a cover you should be aware
that this book is stolen property. It was reported as "unsold and
destroyed" to the publisher, and neither the author nor the
publisher has received any payment for this "stripped book."

STEEPLE HILL BOOKS

Steeple
Hill®

ISBN-13: 978-0-373-44293-5
ISBN-10:   0-373-44293-9

BAYOU PARADOX

Copyright © 2008 by Robin Miller

All rights reserved. Except for use in any review, the reproduction
or utilization of this work in whole or in part in any form by any
electronic, mechanical or other means, now known or hereafter
invented, including xerography, photocopying and recording, or in
any information storage or retrieval system, is forbidden without
the written permission of the editorial office, Steeple Hill Books,
233 Broadway, New York, NY 10279 U.S.A.

This is a work of fiction. Names, characters, places and incidents are
either the product of the author's imagination or are used fictitiously, and
any resemblance to actual persons, living or dead, business establishments,
events or locales is entirely coincidental.

This edition published by arrangement with Steeple Hill Books.

® and TM are trademarks of Steeple Hill Books, used under license.
Trademarks indicated with ® are registered in the United States Patent
and Trademark Office, the Canadian Trade Marks Office and in other
countries.

www.SteepleHill.com

Printed in U.S.A.

I call on you, O God, for you will answer me:
give ear to me and hear my prayer.
—*Psalms* 17:6

For my parents, Joyce & Chuck Bridges—
your belief in me, and unwavering encouragement,
allowed me to seek out the path to follow my dreams.
All my love, Robin

Acknowledgments

My most heartfelt gratitude to…

My talented editor, Krista Stroever, who's so dedicated
to the stories she edits and supportive of her authors.
You rock!

The team at Steeple Hill, who put much time and
energy into all my books.

Kelly Mortimer, for being so much more than just my
agent.

My mentor, Colleen Coble, for continuously teaching
me, but loving me as well.

My prayer group, for lifting me before the throne daily.

My family/friends for invaluable input: BB, Camy,
Cheryl, Dineen, Heather, Lisa, Pammer, Ronie
and Trace. Love y'all.

My family for continued encouragement: Bek, Bubba,
Robert and all the aunts/uncles/cousins/nieces/nephew.
Love each of you.

My daughters—Emily, Remington and Isabella—
the best blessings from God. I love you so much.

All my love to my husband, Case, for his support in
following my dreams and heart.

All glory to my Lord and Savior, Jesus Christ.

ONE

"They've brainwashed you." Tara LeBlanc crossed her arms over her chest and glared at her grandmother. "I can't believe you're turning your back on what you've always believed just because of CoCo and Alyssa's influence." And when Tara had opportunity, she'd tell her sisters exactly what she thought of their tactics. They'd played dirty in this silly game of religious gobbledygook.

Grandmere gave a slow shake of her head, the ends of her gray hair caressing her shoulders. "*Ma chère,* I thought the same thing for many years. Too many. Now, child, it's time to acknowledge the truth."

Tara stared out the kitchen window, chewing the inside of her cheek until she tasted a sharp, coppery tang. How had her sisters duped Grandmere? By getting her so confused she turned away from the voodoo she'd lived, breathed and actively practiced for more than five decades, that's how.

The sunny kitchen darkened as the late-afternoon sun dipped behind the treeline of the bayou. A hush fell over Lagniappe, Louisiana, escorting in the May evening. Tara turned from the window. "I already know the truth. You taught me. I can't believe you've bought into their fairy tale." That fact alone tore Tara's heart.

"So much wasted time. Had I realized how much I needed Jes—"

"Oh, don't start on the preaching stuff. I've heard it enough." And enough, and enough.

"I'm so sorry, *chère*. I've led you wrong."

"No, you haven't. CoCo and Alyssa have just skewed your thinking, is all." She knelt before Grandmere, resting her hands in her grandmother's lap. "Come on out to the work-house with me, yes? We'll mix a cleansing potion and get your head clear." If Tara could just get her grandmother out into the shack beside the house, surely the old ways would beckon her and flush all this nonsense right out of her. *Please, please, come back and teach me, Grandmere.*

"Oh, *ma chère*, I should have that lean-to torn down."

Tara shoved to her feet and planted her fists on her hips, blinking back hot tears of abandonment. "Don't you dare. That's mine now. You may have been hoodwinked, but I sure as shootin' ain't falling for that fantasy trip."

Her heart thudded. Take away her rock of stability? No, she wouldn't let that happen.

"Tara—"

"*Non,* I won't listen anymore. I'm going to clean up the workhouse before I head over to Tanty Shaw's." At least *some*one took over Tara's training to become a voodoo priest-ess. She only mourned that it wasn't Grandmere.

"You'll see, child. God will move in your heart."

Yeah, and so would Santa Claus, the Easter bunny and the tooth fairy, too.

Tara let the kitchen screen door slam behind her. She stomped toward the workhouse, her steps crushing the dried grass. Her stomach twisted into tight knots. For three years she'd studied under her grandmother's tutelage, and because of her sisters' meddling, now she had to continue her studies with someone outside the family. Tradition called for the gift to be passed down from grandmother to granddaughter. Now everything had been ruined. And Tara was the one who suffered.

It was just wrong on so many different levels.

The fishy odor of the bayou drifted on the breeze, tickling Tara's nostrils. The smell reminded her that she needed to gather foliage in the next day or so. If they didn't get rain soon, she'd have to harvest all she could find before the flora died. Tara's stock had slowly diminished since Grandmere had stopped gathering. A lonely sigh escaped.

The rumble of an engine overwhelmed the cacophony of crickets, tree frogs and cicadas readying the bayou for night. She paused at the door of the lean-to, staring out over the waterway. A boat, much too big to maneuver in the tight canals, turned sharply toward the LeBlanc inlet, and suddenly the engine died. The momentum of its surge shoved the boat into the smaller cove.

If the boat kept its course, it'd run right into CoCo's airboat. That would send her oldest sister, currently away on her honeymoon, into a tailspin for sure. What a humdinger to return to—her work craft demolished.

"Hey! Slow down. Use your breaks, *cooyon*. You're gonna hit a boat." She made fast tracks down to the live oak tree anchoring her sister's airboat. "Stop!"

The nose of the big boat veered sharply right, barely missing the end of CoCo's vessel.

Tara popped her fists on her hips as the captain of the big craft moved to the bow deck. "What do you think you're doing? You almost crashed into the airboat."

"Sorry." The man's wide smile diminished his apology. "Didn't realize what a tight fit it'd be."

"Who are you and what are you doing here? This is private property."

"The bayou's privately owned?" He glanced around as if waiting for someone to answer his question. Three more people—two men and a woman—appeared on the deck.

Tara gestured at the ground where one of the men jumped, holding a rope. "That land you're standing on belongs to me. State your name and what you're doing here before I grab my shotgun and shoot you for trespassing."

"No need to shoot anybody, I assure you." The captain laughed and stepped off the boat. The marshy ground sucked in his foot, sloshing water over his pristine white sneakers. Tara bit back a laugh. He gave a shrug and extended his hand. "Name's Vincent Marsalis, and I'm with Winn Pharmaceuticals. We're a research team sent to—"

A pharmaceutical company! "You're trespassing. Get off my property. Now!" Her heart thudded anew. How many times had companies sent out research teams who only damaged the precious plant life? Well, not now. Not on *her* land.

"I don't think you understand. See, we're he—"

"I don't need to understand. You're trespassing, and I'm ordering you to leave. Go." She grabbed the cell phone from her shorts pocket. "I'll call the sheriff."

Vincent What's-His-Name held up both hands in mock surrender. "We don't mean any harm."

"I'll give you till the count of three." She pressed a button, turning on the phone. "One…two…"

"Hey, we're not here to cause trouble."

"Three." Tara jabbed numbers.

"Okay, we'll leave." Vincent nodded at the other man while taking a step backward.

She flipped the phone shut. "And don't come back."

"So much for Southern hospitality," the woman on the deck muttered, her accent making it all too clear she came from up North. Way up North.

"Not when it comes to you meddling Yankees." Tara narrowed her eyes, making sure the group moved quickly.

The engine roared to life. Murky bayou waters swished as reverse engaged, and the boat inched backward. The nose was brought around, then the engine revved. A high arc of water rooster-tailed in the craft's wake. Tara waited until the vessel sped out of sight.

The sun had since melted into the horizon. If she hurried, she could make it to Tanty's before the moon ambled to center sky. At least she didn't have to work at the jazz club tonight. Numbers and accounting didn't hold much interest for her at the moment. She dug out her car keys as she rushed along the gravel path. The evening breeze kissed her flaming face. When would she stop letting people get her so worked up?

Maybe when her life made sense again.

Normally the drive to Tanty's took a good fifteen minutes. Tonight, she made it in less than ten. Pretty good time, considering the condition of her car. Of course, irritation had pushed her foot a little harder on the accelerator. She patted the cracked vinyl of the dashboard. The Mustang might be old and in need of some cosmetic work, but she'd paid for it herself and loved the thing.

Lights from Tanty's workhouse caught in the crystal prisms hanging from the windows, sending colors across the darkened bayou. Tara grabbed her backpack and tossed it over her shoulder. Tanty viewed voodoo not only as a way of life, but also as a business. Her workhouse, three times the size of Grandmere's—no, now Tara's—boasted shrubs along the outer walls and a fresh paint job. Nice blue paint, to keep the bad spirits at bay.

"*Bonjour,* Tanty. Where are you?" Tara stuck her head inside the door. The stench of burnt roots stung her nose. "Tanty?"

No response.

Tara glanced over the tables and stations. A beaker sat atop a burner, the glass bottom singed black. Holding her breath, she flipped off the gas and grabbed an oven mitt. She lifted the container carefully and moved it to the counter.

Something brushed against Tara's leg. She jumped, bumping the metal file cabinet with her hip. A couple of pieces of paper drifted to the floor.

Meow.

Tara laughed and lifted the black cat. She scratched under his chin just the way he liked. "Hey, Spook. Know where Tanty's hiding?"

Spook purred and nudged her hand with his nose.

With a final rub, she lowered the cat to the counter. A drawer sat ajar in the cabinet. Had she bumped the cabinet so hard it opened? She shoved it shut, but not before another piece of paper fluttered to the floor. Tara retrieved all the loose scraps, glancing at them before she put them back in the drawer. Client notes.

Something wasn't right. Tanty kept meticulous records of business transactions, people she'd helped and money she'd taken in. Everything was fanatically filed. Shrewd but smart, that was Tanty Shaw. Why were these not filed properly?

Tara inspected the building a final time. No sign of her mentor. Maybe Tanty had to take a call. Probably in the house, the lit burner totally forgotten. Tanty still had a sharp mind, but she'd passed the seventy-year mark this past April. Only natural she'd get distracted sometimes.

Tara left the workhouse open to air out the scorched odor and strode to the back of Tanty's house. She rapped on the frame of the screen door twice before yanking it open. "Tanty? You in here?"

Silence. Each step Tara made, fear caused her lungs to burn like she'd just jogged a five mile sprint. She moved from the kitchen into the living room. "Tanty?"

A strong weight of oppression stretched across Tara's shoulders, stealing her breath. She closed her eyes. In an instant, the feeling left her.

Peeking around the room, Tara took in the neat and organized space. Not a single thing out of place. Orderly, eerily so, but still no sign of the elderly woman.

Tara took cautious steps down the hall. The wood floor creaked. "Tanty?" Past the bathroom—empty. Past the library—empty. The master bedroom. Her hands cramped as she pushed the door open a crack. "Tanty?"

She took one step into the room. Her heart dropped to her knees.

"Tanty!" Tara rushed to the fallen form on the woven rug. She lifted the limp upper body, dragging the woman's head into her lap. "Tanty!" Her fingers quivered as she pressed hard against her mentor's neck. Very weak pulse.

Ice cloaked her and her stomach churned. She scooted across the floor, reaching for the phone.

Blue strobe lights flashed against the live oaks lining the drive up to his aunt's house. An ambulance met him on the dirt road, then flew past, heading into Lagniappe. Sheriff Bubba Theriot struggled to keep his emotions in check. He needed to remain professional, distance himself from the fact that the victim happened to be his relative. He brought the

cruiser to a stop with a skid before slamming the gear into
Park. Stirred dust settled over the windshield and hood, pro-
viding a fine layer of brown. They needed rain. Soon.

Deputy Gary Anderson cleared his throat. Loudly. "Boss,
I can handle this one for ya if you want to head on over to
the hospital. Will probably be nothing for us to do except
file a report."

Bubba shook his head and reached for the door handle.
"It's my job. I'm fine." Although he didn't feel fine—his gut
was clenched tighter than the worn grip on his service Beretta.
Hadn't the mayor of Lagniappe phoned just last week, demanding that crime in their town be extinguished? All crime,
period. And now Bubba'd been called to the scene of another
incident—a woman unconscious for no apparent reason.

Aunt Tanty.

At least her illness didn't involve foul play. But when a
woman, no matter how old, just fell unconscious, a report had
to be filed. Not to mention the 9-1-1 call required a follow-up
report. Could be a break in a gas main, which could put the
good citizens of Lagniappe in danger. He quickened his pace
up the stairs to Tanty's house, the deputy dogging his heels.

The front door stood open. Even from the foyer, he could
make out low murmuring coming from Tanty's bedroom. He
nodded at Anderson and strode quickly down the hall. Pictures
of his family, himself included, lined the darkened walls.
Bubba swallowed the lump in his throat and reached his aunt's
room.

Tara LeBlanc was slumped on the floor against the master
bed, her eyes closed and her lips moving. As an officer of the
law, he had to observe body language and what people didn't
say. He could detect nothing but concentration from the
youngest LeBlanc. But concentrating on what?

He squatted beside her, laying a hand on her shoulder. She startled, peering at him with those wide eyes of hers. Orbs so dark they reminded him of smooth chocolate—the kind Aunt Tanty always had hidden in the back of the pantry. Bubba shifted his weight to the balls of his feet, an old injury causing a cramp. "Tara."

Hard lines shadowed the corners of her eyes. "I found her like that. Just…just lying there…unconscious."

"I know." His voice cracked as emotion clogged his throat. He swallowed, hard. "We'll get a report from the hospital as soon as possible." He squeezed her shoulder. "I need you to come into the living room now."

He cupped his hand under her elbow and gently urged her to stand. "Just a couple of questions."

She kept her hands splayed open as she moved down the hall. Bubba led her toward the living room. She swayed every couple of steps. Tara LeBlanc might be many things, but weird topped the list.

He helped her to the couch. She plopped onto it, all the while shaking her head and mumbling, "Tanty has to be all right. I just talked to her this morning. She didn't mention not feeling well."

Duty called, despite his tangled emotions. Bubba pulled out his notebook and sat on the edge of the chair adjacent to her. He licked the tip of his pencil. "What time this morning did you talk to Tanty?"

Tara blinked several times before focusing on his face. "Around ten or so. I'd called to ask her a question."

"About what?"

"A potion."

The voodoo stuff. His heart sank. His aunt had never accepted the free gift of salvation. What if she didn't regain consciousness in the hospital? Regret pushed bile into the back of his throat. "I see." What else could he say?

Tara's eyes narrowed as she studied him. "I know you're into all that church stuff like my family, but you don't have to be so obvious in your disapproval of others' way of life."

He gripped the pencil so hard it was a wonder the instrument didn't snap in two. *Just let it go.* "Why'd you come here?"

"I've been training under Tanty."

Right. He remembered now. Mrs. LeBlanc, Tara's grandmother, had just recently accepted Jesus into her heart. He'd heard she joined CoCo's church a couple of months ago. Too bad his aunt had stepped in as a replacement role model for the youngest LeBlanc. "What time did you arrive?"

"About nine or so."

"Did you notice anything out of place?"

She popped her knuckles. Ah, a sign of distress. "She'd left a burner on in the workhouse. The roots had dried up and burned."

"That's unusual?" He avoided his aunt's shed like the plague. Creeped him out.

"For Tanty it is. And there were some loose papers in her file cabinet. Not like her at all. She's very fanatical about her workstation being kept in pristine condition." She glanced around the living room. "Like she is about her house."

A memory pressed forward in his mind: Him, as a teen, rushing into the house to tell Aunt Tanty about making first string in football. He'd forgotten all about his dirty cleats. But not his aunt. Oh, but no. She'd hollered at him to take those "muddy clodhoppers" to the back porch. But she'd listened and commented on his accomplishment with excitement— while he swept and mopped her wooden floors.

"When I didn't find her in the workhouse, I came here to look for her."

He'd almost let memory lane distract him from doing his job. Maybe he should have Anderson take over. No. He owed it to Aunt Tanty to find out what happened. "Do you have a key?"

"I do, but didn't have to use it. The kitchen door was open."

Like most people in Lagniappe, his aunt often left doors unlocked. "You didn't move anything in the house, did you?"

"No, except I pushed open the bedroom door. Oh, and I used the phone in her bedroom to call your office." She shook her head. "I didn't even think to use my cell."

He glanced over the room. No sign of a struggle, no forced entry. He breathed a sigh, glad he wouldn't have to answer to the mayor on this call.

"Someone did this to her, you know."

He jerked his attention back to Tara. "What?"

"She didn't just fall down. Someone set out to hurt her."

"Why do you say that?"

She met his stare head-on. "I can feel the spirits here."

Great. The spirits. Such reliable eye-witnesses.

Lord, please give me strength.

TWO

"Grandmere, Grandmere. Where are you?" Tara let the kitchen screen door slam closed.

"Coming, child."

Grandmere shuffled into the kitchen and grasped the back of a chair. "What's put a bee in your bonnet?"

"It's Tanty Shaw. She's been taken to the hospital."

"Oh, mercy me!" Grandmere's long hair stuck out at odd angles from her head. The belt on her robe hung slack. "What happened, *ma chère?*"

Tara shook her head. "I found her unconscious in her bedroom."

"What'd the doctor say?"

"They took her to the hospital. The sheriff was headed there when he left her house."

"The sheriff? That poor boy." Grandmere shook her head.

Poor boy? Funny, he didn't impress Tara as someone who needed sympathy. He'd been strong and dutiful. And rather strong and handsome, too, although she wouldn't admit that little fact. She'd known the sheriff since she was a toddler and never thought him handsome. Why now? Tara shook her head and answered her grandmother. "I called 9-1-1, and he came. Showed up right after the ambulance left with Tanty."

"Did he say anything? Was anything amiss?"

"Not really. But Tanty had left a burner on in her workhouse and loose papers about."

"That's not like her. Has she been acting daft?"

"No."

"Maybe she had a heart attack." Grandmere's hand fluttered to her chest, and her face paled. Probably remembering her own heart attack a little over a year ago.

"No, someone did this to her."

"Who? What?"

"I don't know, but I intend to find out."

"But if she was unconscious, how do you know?" Her grandmother's expression softened. "Sometimes health conditions aren't easily detected, child."

"No, I *know* someone did this to her."

"How?"

"I felt it, Grandmere. I sat on the floor where I found her, and I knew. The spirits told me."

Grandmere's lips pressed into a straight line and her brow furrowed. "Tara Leigh LeBlanc, you listen to me. I was wrong to ever teach you such evil things. That I did is on my heart. You're messin' with some dangerous stuff, and you need to stop. Right now."

Tara felt as if her heart had been gripped in a vise. "No, you weren't wrong. It's working, Grandmere. I can hear them…feel them. They want to help me find out who did this to Tanty."

"Those spirits are not of God. You stop treading where—"

Tara held up her hands. "Enough. I don't want to hear about God for the umpteenth time. Fine. I get it. You're all gaga over that stuff. Believe what you want, and I'll do the same."

She spun to the sink and twisted the tap on high. How could her grandmother just ignore what she'd practiced for a lifetime?

Water spurted into the porcelain sink, drowning out her grandmother's words. Tara grabbed a glass with shaking hands and shoved it under the stream, then gulped down the cool water. Why couldn't things have just stayed the same? And even though Grandmere had turned away from voodoo, she had to at least acknowledge the practice was real. Why wouldn't she discuss what Tara knew the spirits had told her?

Small beams of light outside the window grabbed her attention, and she turned the knob slowly to cut off the water. "Grandmere, someone's in the bayou."

"Oh, yes. A nice young man came by after you left and asked if he could gather a little foliage for some type of research his company is conducting."

That Yankee from the pharmaceutical company! Tara didn't bother replying to her grandmother. She snatched a flashlight from the top of the icebox, shoved open the screen door and hurried across the uneven ground, littered with half-buried tree roots. *Research, my foot.* Hadn't she made it clear he wasn't welcome? She punctuated her steps with venomous thoughts. She *so* wasn't in the mood to deal with such *cooyons*—stupid people—twice in one day.

She pushed through the underbrush, ignoring the thorns and brambles scraping against her bare legs. The beam of her flashlight bounced off the parched and cracked ground. Idiotic people to be out in the bayou at night. Were they trying to get themselves killed? Her sister's pet alligator, Moodoo, loved to hang around this part of the swampland. Didn't these imbeciles understand that the bayou's wildlife came alive at night? Most were reptiles, and not at all friendly.

"Hey!"

Beams of light shot to her face, blinding her. She stopped and shielded her eyes with her hand. "Move your lights, will ya?"

The rays fell to the ground. Tara continued stomping toward the group of four. "What're y'all doing here?" She glared at the leader, whatever his name was. "Didn't I tell you today you weren't welcome on my land? Was I unclear?"

He flashed his row of pearly whites. "We talked to your grandmother, I believe she is, and she gave us permission to be here."

Tara sucked in air. His smiling really got on her nerves. "Consider this my revoking of that permission."

"Now, now, little lady, we're just gathering some plants and will be on our way. What's the harm?"

Little lady? Chauvinistic *cooyon!* She gripped the flashlight tighter. "Besides the fact that you're just asking to get bit by a snake or gator?" She shook her head. "Never mind. I'm telling you to get off my land one last time."

"Snakes?" The woman in the group sidled up beside him. Her chic hair shimmered in the near darkness. "Maybe we should leave."

"Yeah, maybe you should." Tara flashed her beam of light to the other two men. They held little cloth bags with leaves peeking out. Desecrating *her* bayou. She curled her free hand into a tight fist. "Now would be smart."

"I think we have enough anyway, boss," one of the other men mumbled.

Tara shot her light to the leader's face—what was his name? "Why are y'all out here at night, anyway? What are you hiding? What're you really doing?"

"Come on, Vincent. Let's just get out of here." The woman clung to his arm, her red polished nails glimmering. A model lookalike was part of a pharmaceutical research team?

Vincent—that was his name—shrugged off the woman's grip. "Like I told you, we're just gathering some samples to run a few tests."

"Mmm-hmm." Tara ground her teeth. "You have to just go."

"No need to be rude." The woman tossed her blond hair defiantly.

"Hannah." Vincent took the woman's elbow and nodded at Tara. "Forgive us. We'll head out now."

"And don't come back again or I'll call the police."

He stared at her for a long moment before giving her a curt nod and leading the others through the bayou toward the canal. Interesting that they didn't come into the offshoot the way they had earlier. Were they sneaking in? What were they really up to? Reputable research teams didn't skulk around the swamp at night.

She waited until the roar of their boat engine grew faint and then headed back to the house. What had Grandmere been thinking, granting them permission? It was that new religion stuff. Three months ago, Grandmere would've protected the plants in the bayou like a lioness protecting her cubs. Now she wasn't even concerned about what she once cared most about.

All due to the meddling of her sisters.

The moon rushed from cloud to cloud. Too bad the billows weren't heavy with rain. Lagniappe needed rain something fierce.

Tara wiped her feet on the rug before entering the kitchen. She eased the screen door closed, not wanting to disturb

Grandmere if she'd gone back to bed. She treaded lightly across the wooden floor, which creaked, anyway, into the living room.

"I called the hospital to check on Tanty."

Tara jumped at her grandmother's voice. "I thought you'd gone to bed."

"*Non,* not with my friend in the hospital, *ma chère.*"

"What'd they say?" Tara plopped on the threadbare couch beside her grandmother.

"Just that her condition hasn't changed. She's still in a coma. René's with her."

"Who's René?"

Grandmere chuckled. "The sheriff."

Tara snorted. Big macho cop stuck with such a feminine name, even if it was a throwback to his French ancestors. "No wonder everybody calls him Bubba." She couldn't help but recall how the pain had flickered in his eyes when he'd talked to her about Tanty. Kind. Caring. Gentle. Wait a minute, she didn't want to think of him like that. Her voice lost all trace of laughter. "Grandmere, I don't want those people on our land anymore. Respectable research teams don't sneak in and pillage leaves under cover of darkness."

"I didn't realize they'd be out there at night when they asked, child. Pharmaceutical companies have been sending people out here for plants and such ever since I can remember. They take a couple of samples and go on their merry way. It's normal."

"But not these. Please, Grandmere, don't give them permission if they ask again."

The old woman nodded and struggled to her feet. "They probably won't show up again, anyway." She groaned under her breath. "I'm going to bed now. *Bonsoir.*"

Tara waited until her grandmother shuffled down the hall into her bedroom before she decided to raid the icebox. Adrenaline wouldn't allow her to sleep just yet. She bit into a fried chicken leg, holding it with her teeth as she grabbed a soda. She stood at the sink, eating her late-night snack without really tasting the cayenne pepper tingling her taste buds, and mulling over the day's events.

Tanty's condition wasn't a sudden illness. Someone had deliberately harmed her. Tara was sure of it. She tossed the bone into the trash, gulped down the last of the soda, then disposed of the can. She'd find out who was behind this attack on Tanty. And she knew just where to start.

Her shed. It was time to do some conjuring.

The morning sun crested over the line of the trees surrounding the hospital. From his perch in the ICU waiting room on the fourth floor, Bubba witnessed the purple streaks giving way to orange. Breathtaking, really. He had to concentrate on something—anything besides where he stood. The last time he'd been in this hospital, he'd been a patient. On this very floor, fighting for his life. He'd gotten too close to an arms-smuggling ring, and had been beaten and left for dead in the middle of a road. If Alyssa LeBlanc, Tara's sister, hadn't come along when she did... Not exactly a happy memory.

He turned from the window and glanced at the clock on the wall. Five more minutes and the staff would let him see Aunt Tanty. The nurses had kept him updated during the night on his aunt's condition. No change. Preliminary tests gave no indications of the cause of her illness. He prayed for the best.

Prayed hard.

He blinked burning eyes. Wearing contacts for only a

couple of months, he still hadn't gotten accustomed to his eyes drying out. He dug in his pocket for his contact solution and administered a few drops. After his visit, he'd run home and take a quick shower, grab a bite and then head into the office. He'd have to file his report, and he hadn't a clue what to say. He knew nothing. Natural causes? People didn't just fall into a coma, did they? The gas company representative would be at Aunt Tanty's this morning to inspect for leaks. Maybe he'd get a clue from that. Either way, he'd make sure he returned to the hospital in time for a noon visit with his aunt.

"Sheriff."

He spun toward the door to the waiting room, expecting to see one of the nurses informing him it was time for his fifteen minutes with Aunt Tanty. Instead, Tara LeBlanc stood there. Weird, yes, but she sure looked pretty framed by the doorway.

He shook his head to clear the thought. Must be sleep deprivation. "Yes?"

"How is she?"

"The same. I get to visit her in a few minutes."

Tara nodded, her dark hair brushing her shoulders, and crossed to him. "Have they said what caused this?"

The questions behind her perceptive eyes matched his own. "They're running various tests."

"Someone did this to her."

Bubba ran a tongue over his teeth, wishing at times like this he hadn't given up dipping. "We'll get to the bottom of it."

"You going into the office today?"

"After I see Aunt Tanty."

"I'll stay here and call you if there's any change."

He offered her his first genuine smile. "You don't have to do that. The nurse will page me."

"I'd like to stay for a while. Maybe get to see her." Her voice held an edge of determination...and hope.

"Sure."

"I need to come by the station later, anyway."

"Oh, you don't have to do that. I already have your statement." He looked at her for a moment.

She set her chin and shook her head. "This is something else. I need to report trespassers, file a complaint or something."

"Trespassing? Where?" He reached automatically for his notebook and pencil.

"The bayou. LeBlanc property."

"When?" He jotted down a note.

"Yesterday and then again last night."

He stopped writing. "Last night?"

"By flashlight. Gathering plants. They say they're with some pharmaceutical company doing research."

Oh. Nothing to get excited about. Bubba slipped the notebook back into his pocket. "Fairly common around here. You should know that."

"After midnight? After I'd already told them to get off my property?"

He let out a long breath and caught sight of a nurse waving at him from the doorway. "You can come by and file a complaint, but chances are, they won't be back. If you'll excuse me, it's time for my visit with Aunt Tanty."

Following the nurse down the hallway, Bubba pondered Tara's adamant claim that someone had made his aunt sick. From training, he knew some criminals tried to "help" the police as a way to assuage their guilt. Others just wanted to get caught. Was Tara one of those?

He shook off the preposterous idea and stepped into his aunt's room. Machines beeped and hummed, filling him with dread. Those were the first sounds he'd heard when he'd regained consciousness. Then his best friend's voice.

Bubba slipped into the bedside chair and gripped his aunt's hand. How paper-thin her skin felt. "Aunt Tanty." His words came out as a croak. He cleared his throat. "Aunt Tanty, I'm here."

Her face didn't change. Her hand didn't squeeze his. Could she hear him? He recalled bits and pieces of his own time in a coma. Snatches of voices, pinpricks of conversation.

Would any of that seep into his aunt's conscious mind? Maybe, maybe not. But he knew God was still on the throne and still in the miracle business.

He leaned closer to his aunt's ear. "I love you, Aunt Tanty. But someone else loves you even more. For once, I'm not going to remain silent. You're going to listen to me about Jesus. About salvation. About eternal life."

THREE

Lifeless.

That was how Tanty appeared, lying so still in the hospital bed. After the sheriff left, Tara decided to wait for the next visiting time to see her mentor. Now she kept vigil as the beeps and blips from the machines attached to Tanty kept a droning rhythm.

Tara swallowed against a mouth as dry as the bayou right now. *Just open your eyes, Tanty. Look at me.*

But the woman didn't move an eyelid. So still. The tube down her throat rasped as the machine kept her breathing. Goose bumps pimpled Tara's arms as she stared at the IV drip. If only Tanty could swallow. Tara had a healing potion in her purse, but no way to get it into Tanty's system. Dare she try to slip some into the bag hanging from the pole?

Tests being run? Right. They'd only look for natural causes for Tanty's condition. But Tara knew better. Someone had deliberately done this. If the police wouldn't investigate properly, then she would.

She squeezed Tanty's hand a final time before planting a kiss on the woman's thinning hair and rushing from the room. Tara blinked away hot tears as she passed the nurses' station.

Somebody was responsible, and Tara would make sure they paid.

The Louisiana sun beat down on Lagniappe as Tara drove to Tanty's house. Those client records being out of the filing cabinet had bothered her all night while she brewed the healing potion. Tanty never left documentation of her clients' identities just lying around in the open. Never. She considered it a violation of their privacy. She'd never even shown real ones to Tara, only ones she'd filled out in order to teach accurate record-keeping.

Tara would start her investigation in the workhouse with those files. Might be considered invading someone's privacy, but she needed answers.

Voodoo practice demanded justice for Tanty.

So did Tara.

The old homestead stood as still and quiet as it had when the police had left last night. Tara glanced around before making her way to the shed. She'd locked it up last night with the sheriff before she left. Her key turned easily in the lock.

A trace of the burning stench lingered in the close, still room. Tara opened the windows and propped open the door. Being there without Tanty felt wrong. Very wrong. She shoved off the eerie sensation, opened the filing cabinet and pulled out the three client sheets she'd secured yesterday.

Meow!

The cat jumped onto the counter, tail twitching.

"Oh, Spook, I'm so sorry. I bet nobody remembered to feed you." She grabbed the bag of cat food from the cabinet and shook some into his bowl, then filled his water basin. "I'm sorry," she whispered as she gave his back a rub. The cat ignored her, digging into his food.

Dropping onto a stool, Tara studied the first piece of paper.

Under the date, not even thirty days ago, the following information was penned in Tanty's neat block letters:

> Suzie Richard. Female issue. Discussed options. Recommended to physician. Client became distraught, not wanting husband to know and medical procedure won't allow for total discretion. Denied further requests from client.

Tara reread the notes. Distraught, huh? Suzie Richard, Suzie Richard…Tara couldn't bring a face to the name. She grabbed the phone book from Tanty's desk and looked under R. No Suzie Richard in the book. Probably listed under her husband's name. Where had Tara heard the name before?

She'd come back to that. Tara turned the paper facedown on the desk and read from the second client sheet, also dated last month.

> Melvin Dubois. Three treatments of formula 12. All failed. Recommended therapy to assist. Client upset treatments failed, although explained he had to work with treatments to overcome. Referred from Marie. Severed further communication with client.

Tara remembered him. He'd been to see Grandmere several times in the months leading to Alyssa and CoCo's brainwashing of their grandmother. What for? He'd been upset? She'd have to ask Grandmere about him when she got home.

Flipping to the last client sheet, she noted it was also dated April.

Rebekah Carlson. One treatment of formula 38. Wonderful results. Client pleased, but expressed concerns when another client witnessed her leaving. Will schedule any future appointments with her to avoid her being seen on the premises.

Tara glanced out the window facing the bayou. Most people didn't talk about their voodoo treatments, but it wasn't exactly a huge secret in Lagniappe. If she had to guess, she'd say at least forty percent of the townspeople had sought out a priestess for some sort of treatment.

Hold the presses! Rebekah Carlson…*Mayor* Carlson's wife? Respected pillar of the community? Oh, my, no wonder Mrs. Carlson was so concerned about someone seeing her. Tara glanced back at the note. Formula 38. Now, which one was that treatment for? She'd have to use Tanty's master ledger.

Gravel crunched in the driveway. Tara jumped to her feet and stared out the window in front of the house. A police cruiser rolled to a stop, followed by a truck with the gas company's logo. Tara quickly unlocked the desk drawer, grabbed the master ledger and shoved it and the three pieces of paper into her backpack. She slammed down the windows and pulled the door behind her just as Deputy Anderson paused by her car.

"What're you doing here, Ms. LeBlanc?"

"Just came by to get some of my things I'd left here." She took deliberate steps to her Mustang. Spook whooshed through the cat door and scampered off into the bayou. "And I needed to feed Tanty's cat. Poor thing's bowl was empty."

"Uh, you shouldn't be around here anymore. Not until the sheriff clears it."

She tossed her backpack into the passenger seat through the open window and crossed her arms over her chest. "Is this a crime scene now?" Maybe, just maybe, they'd gotten a test result back and the sheriff would take her seriously now.

"Not exactly, but until we're sure there's no gas leak or something, you need to steer clear of the area."

Tara snorted and slipped behind the steering wheel. It figured they would still blow off her beliefs. "I'm not going to let the cat starve. I'll be leaving now, but I'll come back tomorrow to feed Spook."

The deputy stared at her as she turned the car and headed home. She glanced in her rearview mirror and found him still standing in the driveway. Probably wondering if he should've inspected her pack.

Too late. They wouldn't know what to do with the information, anyway.

Her stomach rumbled as she parked in front of her house. She'd skipped breakfast, wanting to get to the hospital to check on Tanty. Grandmere had said she'd make crawfish-stuffed *pistolettes* for lunch, and Tara's mouth watered at the thought. She bounded up the creaking stairs and flew into the house.

No enticing smell greeted her. The house stood as silent as a tomb.

Tara stuck her head into the kitchen and took in the scene. Counters wiped clean. Cabinets shut tight. Towel neatly folded by the stove.

Nope, Grandmere hadn't even made the preparations for the *pistolettes*. Very odd. They weren't exactly something whipped up in less than fifteen minutes. The coffeepot's "on" button glowed. Tara punched it off. Two coffee cups sat in the sink beside two plates and forks. Grandmere'd obviously had company this morning. Who?

"Grandmere," Tara called as she headed down the hall.

No reply. A freaky sense of déjà vu crept over Tara. So similar to…yesterday.

Quickening her pace, Tara called out again. "Grandmere. Where are you?" She pushed open her grandmother's door. The bed, neatly made, sat empty, just like the rest of the room.

The icy chill returned, settling between her shoulder blades. Her head pounded as her pulse spiked. She flew into the hall, her feet moving of their own volition.

Tara rushed to the bathroom. The door was cracked. She pushed it fully open. "Grandmere?"

Her heart leaped into her throat. Her grandmother lay sprawled over the sink. Tara ran forward and eased the old woman into her lap. "Noooo!"

She felt desperately for a pulse against the panic and fear hammering in her chest.

Faint and thready, but detectable.

Again the cold encased Tara's heart, and the feeling came through loud and clear—someone had done this to Grandmere.

She reached for the cell phone in her pocket but kept her eyes glued to Grandmere's face.

Her colorless, unconscious face.

The late afternoon sun kissed the top of the hospital's roof. The sheriff stared into the sky, his thoughts and emotions uneasy. Another elderly Lagniappe citizen had fallen into a coma for no apparent reason.

Bubba entered the hospital again, his mind reeling. No test results had come back on why his aunt had lost consciousness, and now Marie LeBlanc had been rushed to the hospital with the same strange illness barely twenty-four hours later. Something was going on in his town, and he intended to find out what. He headed to the nurses' station outside the emergency room.

"Sheriff."

It was Tara LeBlanc. She stood in the hallway, her eyes red and puffy. Her long hair was captured in a ponytail at the nape of her neck, spilling over her shoulder and down her back. She looked delicate, alone. His heart tugged and he took her arm. "How's your grandmother?"

"Unconscious." She pulled free of his grip.

"Did the paramedics indicate any reason? Maybe she had another heart attack?" The old woman'd had one a year or so ago.

"No. They have her on a monitor now, but the preliminary EKG shows it wasn't her heart. She's just unconscious. Sound familiar?" Her soft tone now shifted to downright sarcastic.

Anxious enough himself, he reached into his pocket for his notebook and pencil. He'd just ignore the tone. Better to keep it all business. Despite the fact that even under duress she still struck a chord in him. One that made him want to hug her and comfort her, protect her. "I'll need to ask you a few questions. Do you have a minute now, or do you need to be with your grandmother?"

"They're preparing her to move up to ICU, so I'm fine. But your questions aren't going to do any good. The door was open to the house when I got home. Nothing had been disturbed. I found Grandmere just lying over the sink in the bathroom." Her voice cracked on the last sentence, the sarcasm giving way to fear and worry.

"Where had you been?"

She hauled in a breath, releasing it with a slight hiss. "At Tanty's."

What? He stared at her. "Whatever for?"

"I, uh, needed to feed Spook. I didn't even go into the house. Deputy Anderson and the guy from the gas company got there just as I was leaving."

"Stay away from there for now."

"The cat has to be fed."

"I'll take care of him."

"I have a key. It's not like I broke in or anything." Her tone resembled a child's defensive whine.

The thought occurred to him again—could she know something and subconsciously be trying to tell him?

Her big brown eyes filled with unshed tears. No, she'd never do anything to hurt Tanty, much less her own grandmother.

Time to bring the subject back in hand. "Did you notice anything unusual at your house?"

"Already told you, no." She popped her knuckles. "Well, somebody must have visited Grandmere this morning because there were two cups and plates in the sink. She hadn't mentioned anyone planning to come by."

"Was that unusual? People just dropping in to say hello?"

"Clients used to quite a bit, but ever since Grandmere *found God,* the only people who show up are church folk."

Her animosity wasn't hard to miss, but he let it go. This had to be extremely trying for her. Especially since CoCo and Luc were on their honeymoon and Alyssa and Jackson lived in New Orleans. Basically, she would have to handle a serious situation on her own. "I'll need to come by and check things out later."

She shrugged. "The house is unlocked. Be my guest to poke around. You won't find anything."

He'd argue the point, but chances were he'd find just what he'd found at Aunt Tanty's—zilch. A big fat nothing.

"This isn't a coincidence, Sheriff." Her sharp tone brought his focus to her.

"I'll be investigating what happened to your grandmother, Tara." He kept his voice low, his tone even. Professional. Authoritative. Well, at least he hoped that was how he sounded.

She huffed out a breath. "Like you're investigating what happened to Tanty?"

He didn't take offense. She would lash out at everyone. Perfectly natural response. "We're running every possible test to find out what caused these symptoms, I assure you."

"But will it be in time to save them?" Her voice caught and she sniffled. "They're just lying there, wasting away."

"Tanty's my aunt. Of course, I'm doing everything I can to get to the bottom of this." His heart twisted. Didn't Tara realize it hurt him just as much to see his aunt lying there like that? "The medical staff is doing everything it can."

"That's not good enough." She grabbed his forearm. His muscles tensed automatically and his heart picked up its pace at her touch. "We need to find out who did this to them."

She released her hold on his arm, but his heart continued to race. No, he wouldn't allow himself to be sidetracked from the matter at hand. Couldn't. Back to the facts. They were something he could control. Black and white. Cut and dried.

"Someone did this, Sheriff. I know it." Her voice held a pleading tone. "We need to find out who's responsible."

How could someone have done this, caused two elderly women to just lose consciousness? It didn't make sense. More than likely, there was a logical explanation. Something the team of doctors would find and be able to treat. Heal. "We'll know more once the test results are in."

A nurse emerged from behind a curtain, her white shoes squeaking against the tile floor, and addressed Tara. "Ms. LeBlanc, we're moving your grandmother now. You can go up to the fourth floor and see the nurses for her visitation schedule."

"Merci." Tara turned back to him, her eyes hard and unwavering. "Fine, you keep running tests and looking for medical answers. I'll find out who's behind this on my own."

"Tara, don't stir up anything." Wasn't that what voodoo was all about, stirring up spirits and potions?

"What could I possibly stir up, Sheriff? This is all perfectly reasonable, totally logical, right?"

"Stay out of it. Take care of your grandmother, and let the police handle the investigation." He didn't give her a chance to reply, just strode down the hall.

Infuriating woman. Yet striking. Strong, but vulnerable. A true enigma. One who, despite his better judgment, seemed to draw him to her.

In spite of all her rough edges, she loved her grandmother and his aunt dearly. It was only her concern for them that made her act like this.

At least, he hoped that was the reason. Surely she couldn't be right.

But what if she was?

He strode into the elevator, jabbed the fourth-floor button and waited as the elevator jerked into motion. Maybe the doctors would have some test results back. Ones with definite answers. Ones that would defy Tara LeBlanc's outrageous allegations.

Barely waiting for the doors to slide fully open, Bubba marched to the ICU nurses' station. The kindly gray-haired nurse from yesterday smiled as he approached. "It's still an hour from your visiting time, Sheriff."

"I need to know if any of the tests on my aunt have come back yet." He rested his elbows on the counter, hunching over to get on eye level with her.

"They're not back yet. I'm sorry."

He shook his head and straightened. "In the meantime, my aunt is just lying there. I want answers, Nurse."

"Careful there, Sheriff. Sounds like you might be considering that something funny's going on," Tara said from behind him. "Sure wouldn't want anyone to get the wrong impression, yes?"

He glared at her over his shoulder. "I'm just checking up on my aunt, as well as trying to conduct a police investigation."

She lifted her chin. "I wasn't aware a *medical* condition warranted a police investigation." Her eyebrows hitched over her stunning eyes. "Sounds like you might suspect I'm right."

He'd never admit that. Not now. Not without facts. He pivoted and crossed his arms over his chest. "I told you I'd run a thorough investigation."

A half smile sneaked onto her face. "I'm impressed."

"Ms. LeBlanc?" a nurse interrupted. "Your grandmother is settled now. You can visit her for fifteen minutes."

Tara nodded, then stared at him again. "Let me know when you face facts and want some help." She turned and followed the nurse down the hall.

Little upstart, as if she could help him with anything. Still, there was something about her. Something brave and…beautiful.

He shoved the thought away, refusing to dwell on Tara LeBlanc. He had his faith, his career and his friends. He didn't have time for romance or a relationship.

And with Tara's belief in voodoo, there was no potential for one.

Or was there?

FOUR

Night fell over Lagniappe in a hush. No storms, no quaking skies, nothing special to signify another day was done.

Tara stared at the phone in her hand, as she'd been doing for nearly half an hour. She needed to call Alyssa, at least, but didn't have enough energy for the fight she knew would ensue. She'd never really gotten along with Alyssa, not like she did with CoCo. Maybe because Alyssa had fled the bayou as soon as she'd been able. She only just began accepting her roots in the past year. Marrying Jackson Devereaux and living in New Orleans probably helped, too. Her sisters deserved to know about Grandmere. Especially if she never recovered. Tara swallowed the thought. That wouldn't happen. She'd already made the healing potion, and would get some of it into Grandmere's system somehow.

If only CoCo weren't on her honeymoon. Tara would much rather deal with her oldest sister than Alyssa, who would load up her husband and head out from New Orleans immediately. She let out a sigh. The phone wouldn't dial itself. Then again, maybe she should wait until tomorrow. Give the potion time to work. Wouldn't it be better to call both couples with more hopeful news than what she had now?

CoCo and Luc. Alyssa and Jackson. Tara, alone.

The cold hard truth hit her square between the eyes like never before. Without Grandmere, she was all alone. No one to talk to, no one to share her fears and burdens with. Life wasn't fair. The need to cry nearly choked her.

She. Would. Not. Feel. Sorry. For. Herself.

The sheriff's face flashed through her mind. Why was that? Tara pinched her eyes closed and shook her head hard.

"No!" She shoved herself to her feet. No more wallowing in self-pity. Starting now, she'd be proactive. She'd find the person responsible for Tanty's and Grandmere's condition, see justice served, then her life could get back to normal. She'd never cared much about men or being in a relationship with one, so what was her problem now? Look at how her sisters had changed their lives to accommodate their husbands—CoCo had to convert to the whole Christian thing, and Alyssa gave up her journalism career to move to New Orleans and marry. If that was what love did to people, she'd pass, thank you very much.

She stalked to the kitchen table and opened her backpack, then carefully set out the three client sheets from Tanty's. The master ledger followed. Tara hunched in the chair, studying the paperwork.

After rereading the note on Rebekah Carlson, Tara looked up formula 38 in the ledger. And nearly fell out of the chair. That was the treatment for male impotency. The mayor suffered from impotency? No wonder Mrs. Carlson went to see Tanty.

Did the mayor know? What if Mrs. Carlson had told him someone saw her leaving? Implications knotted Tara's stomach. How far would Mayor Carlson go to protect his public image, especially over something so private?

Beep! Beep! Beep!

She jumped, disoriented for a second, then pressed off the alarm on her watch. Time to go visit Grandmere. Tara headed to the car, shoving her hand into her pocket to touch the vial. Healing potion good to go.

She turned the key, but the engine didn't respond. Great. She didn't have time for this. Running a hand over the dashboard, she whispered, "Come on, baby." After twisting the key three more times in rapid succession, the engine turned over. She pumped the accelerator several times, letting the engine rev. Whew!

The air conditioner didn't have time to get the car's cabin cooled off before Tara whipped into a parking spot outside the hospital. Too much heat and humidity for an old clunker like her Mustang to overcome. Her damp shirt clung to her back as she made her way through the automatic doors.

Cold air blasted her face. She paused, closing her eyes for a brief moment and relishing the reprieve from the oppressive heat. Only May, and already over ninety degrees. It would be a long hot summer.

Two nurses greeted her as she stepped off the elevator on the fourth floor. They told her there was no change with her grandmother. She fingered the vial in her pocket again—she'd just see about that "no change" status.

Grandmere's face appeared even paler. Worse than when she'd had her heart attack, even. Tara flashed a shaky smile to the nurse exiting the room, clipboard in hand. She glanced over her shoulder. No one stood outside the glass wall of the ICU unit. No one watched her.

She withdrew the vial from her pocket. The machines attached to Grandmere emitted a steady beep. Tara's heartbeat beat in time. She unscrewed the lid and withdrew the dropper. Another glance over her shoulder. Coast still clear.

Tara eased forward and slipped the end of the dropper past her grandmother's cracked lips. She pressed the little bulb, releasing four drops into Grandmere's mouth. And waited. The potion would absorb quickly through the tongue.

Seconds, then minutes ticked off the clock. Tara waited. She closed her eyes and mumbled the voodoo words she'd been taught.

The beeps from the machine broke rhythm—skipping once, doubling in the next second.

Tara opened her eyes and fell silent, staring at her grandmother. There—was that a twitch or had her eyelids quivered?

She repeated the administration of four drops before slipping the vial back into the pocket of her shorts. Grandmere couldn't have more potion until tonight. Would the dosage now be enough to bring her from her coma?

The door behind Tara swished open. She jerked and turned.

"Didn't mean to startle you, Ms. LeBlanc." The doctor, his pristine white coat flapping as he walked, moved to Grandmere's side and inspected the machine. "How's our patient?"

"I think she's looking better. Don't you?"

He cast a serious look in Tara's direction. "While she's in stable condition, there's been no change in her vitals."

Tara stood, fighting to look him in the eye. "What about her tests? Have any results come back?"

"Her heart's fine—she hasn't suffered even a mild attack."

Tara already knew that. "What about the toxicology screen?"

"It'll take a few more days for the results to come back."

"And in the meantime?"

"We monitor and wait."

Not good enough. Same lines they'd been fed about Tanty.

Tara leaned over and gave her grandmother a kiss on her sunken cheek and then strode from the ICU room.

And ran straight into Sheriff Theriot.

His chest was as unmoving as a brick wall. She would have fallen over had he not steadied her. "Whoa, where's the fire?"

Frustration filled her. "I'm sick of this." Tears seared the back of her eyelids.

His brows lowered. "Has something happened with your grandmother? Is there a change?"

"No. She's the same. And I'm getting the same tired answers. That's the problem. Nothing. *Nada.* Zilch."

He laid a hand on her shoulder, and comfort eased through her. "These things take time. They'll find out what's wrong."

She shrugged off his touch. She didn't need comfort from a cop. A Christian one at that, even if his image danced in her mind at the most inopportune times. "Not soon enough. I know someone's responsible, and I need to find out who."

"There's nothing for you to do but be here for your grandmother." He hitched an eyebrow. "And pray."

Tara snorted. "Yeah, you do that. I see it working so well with Tanty." The acidic comment stuck to her tongue, but she couldn't help it. What if she lost both Grandmere and Tanty? *Then* where would she be?

He cleared his throat and scowled. "Have you called your sisters?"

Great. Another hit below the belt. "Not yet."

"You need to let them know, Tara."

"I know." She cleared the frog in her throat. "I'll call them this afternoon. I just don't have any information for them."

"They deserve to know. She's their grandmother, too."

She gritted her teeth. "You don't have to tell me. This is

my family business, Sheriff. I'll handle it." She turned and stomped to the elevator.

Cooyon! As if she didn't know what she should do. But she couldn't help wanting to give the potion a little time to work before she called her sisters. Any improvement would be better than what she could tell them now.

She got off the elevator, crossed the lobby and hit the hospital's double doors. Humidity suffocated her as soon as she crossed the threshold. The late-afternoon sun blasted her as she made her way to the car, gluing her shirt to her back again. She slipped behind the wheel. Hot vinyl seared her bare legs. She winced and fumbled with the keys.

"Ms. LeBlanc! Ms. LeBlanc!"

A woman ran across the parking lot, waving her arms. "Wait, Ms. LeBlanc."

Who was she? Tara didn't recognize her, didn't think she'd even seen her before. The engine turned over and lukewarm air sputtered from the vents. She kept the door open as the woman approached.

Red-faced and panting, the waddling woman reached for the door. "I'm glad I caught you." She jerked her hand free as hot metal made contact with her flesh. "Whew! That's hot!"

Patience had never been Tara's strong suit. "Do I know you?"

"Oh, no. Sorry." The woman's thin brown hair was stuck to the sides of her puffy face. "I'm a member of your grandmother's church. The ladies' group wanted to let you know that we're having a round-the-clock prayer vigil for Mrs. LeBlanc."

Lovely. Just what she didn't need to deal with right now. But these were her grandmother's new friends, and her

Southern upbringing dictated she not be rude. "I'm sure she'll be delighted to know that once she comes out of the coma."

"And we wanted to let you know that someone from the church will be bringing dinner by to you every evening."

"You don't have to do that."

"But we want to. And if you need anything, you give us a holler." The woman passed a business card to Tara. "I'm Suzie, by the way."

Tara took the card, giving it a once-over. A cherub floated in the left corner, while the words *Godly Women* jumped off the card. An e-mail address and phone number were listed beneath. "Uh, thanks."

"I mean that. If there's anything we can do for you, just call that number. Someone's available to answer twenty-four/seven."

Oh, happy day. Time to end this little tête-à-tête. "I appreciate that. Thanks again." Tara eased the door closed. At least the air conditioner blew cooler air now.

She put the car in reverse, still gripping the card. She stared at it for a moment before dropping it into the console. Suzie waved from the parking lot as if they were long-lost best friends. Tara turned the car and pointed it toward home.

Godly woman? More like strange woman.

"Sheriff, I understand two elderly ladies have been hospitalized over the past two days."

Bubba shifted in his chair and doodled as he gripped the phone tighter. "Yes, Mayor. My aunt and Luc Trahan's grandmother-in-law." Was that even a word, *grandmother-in-law?*

"Mrs. LeBlanc is a member of our congregation. Is there something going on I should know about?"

Swallowing back a groan, Bubba dropped the pencil onto

his desk calendar. "We're still waiting for test results on both ladies."

"What I'm asking, Sheriff, is, is there a threat to Lagniappe?" The mayor's curt words matched his tone.

What Bubba wouldn't give to be able to answer that question with certainty. "At this moment, sir, I don't think so."

"You don't *think* so? That's not good enough. I need to know. I have to protect the citizens. They've suffered enough recently." Mayor Carlson's implication cut to the core.

Bubba cringed against the reference. Like he didn't remember? "I understand, sir."

"I'm working behind the scenes to try to bring new life into this town. The last thing I need is to scare off potential industrialists."

"I'll get you an answer as soon as I know something."

"You're the sheriff—light a fire under somebody."

"Yes, sir." But the disconnecting click told him the mayor didn't hear him. Bubba slammed the phone back in its cradle.

He didn't need the added stress of Mayor Carlson breathing down his neck. If he were smart, he'd take a leave of absence and spend his time at his aunt's bedside. Unfortunately he didn't have anyone to take his place. Deputy Gary Anderson was good but still too wet behind the ears to head an investigation. Still, this wasn't really a police investigation, right? Just a follow-up.

Reports sat on the edge of his desk. He grabbed the first folder—Anderson's report from the gas company. No leaks detected at Tanty's house, inside or out.

Bubba closed the folder and rubbed his stubbled chin. Had he shaved this morning? He honestly couldn't remember. Okay, so no gas leak. What else?

Tanty Shaw and Marie LeBlanc. Both hospitalized with the same symptoms. Both elderly. Neither very aggressive or with any known enemies. It had to be something medical, right? Nothing else made sense.

But two women having the same mysterious illness that medical staff couldn't easily explain left too many unanswered questions. That didn't make sense, either.

What was the connection?

He closed his eyes and leaned back in his worn chair. Their ages were close, but so were many others in town. They both lived close to the bayou, but so did a lot of other folks.

Voodoo.

Bubba shot upright and stared at the blank wall. That was the only common denominator between them that ruled out most of the rest of the town.

Only, Marie LeBlanc didn't practice voodoo anymore.

But Tara did.

Ah, Tara. Just her mental image sent strange sensations racing through him. He'd known her almost all her life, but now, something about her made him uncomfortable. He hadn't had a chance to analyze his recent reaction to her yet, but he would. Later. After he figured out what was going on in his town.

Voodoo had to be the connection. He had no clue what all that involved. He'd made it a point to steer clear of such nonsense a long time ago. Maybe it was time he paid more attention.

With a heavy sigh, Bubba lifted the phone. He could think of only one person he could ask, but that person would ask questions about why he wanted to know. Everything could snowball from one phone call.

Unfortunately Tara would be on the receiving end of the avalanche.

He didn't have a choice. He flipped through his Rolodex, found the entry and dialed.

FIVE

That interfering, meddlesome man!

Tara marched into the house, muttering under her breath about Sheriff Bubba Theriot. How dare the man take it upon himself to notify *her* family about Grandmere's illness? He had no right. She'd barely made it home when her cell phone rang and Alyssa lit into her. Now she had to deal with her sister and brother-in-law coming to town. As well, Alyssa had called CoCo on her honeymoon.

Oh, just wait until she saw that man again. She'd give him a piece of her mind, no matter how good-looking he was. Good-looking? She must really be going nuts.

The house needed a cleaning. Dirty coffee cups and plates of Grandmere's still sat in the sink. Tara's wet towels from this morning hung haphazardly across the shower rod, and her paperwork covered the kitchen table. Alyssa could probably handle dirty dishes and wet towels with minimal complaint but not the paperwork—not anything to do with voodoo.

She reached for the ledger, but her gaze fell on the client sheets. Her heart gave a little kick.

Suzie Richard!

Tara scanned the notes again.

Female issue. Discussed options. Recommended to
physician. Client became distraught, not wanting
husband to know and medical procedure won't allow
for total discretion. Denied further requests from client.

Could this be the same Suzie who gave her the business
card outside the hospital?

Tara went out to her car and grabbed the card from the
console. No names listed. Just *Godly Women,* an e-mail
address and a phone number. Why hadn't she used the good
manners Grandmere taught her and gotten the woman's last
name?

Returning to the house, Tara stared at Tanty's comments
on the client sheets. Just how distraught was Suzie? Hmm.
She glanced at the card again. Might not even be the same
person. Then again, maybe the name sounded familiar
because Grandmere'd mentioned Suzie when talking about
her church group. Could be a long shot, but it was the best
lead she had at the moment.

She could lose Grandmere and Aunt Tanty. The enormity
and severity of the situation hit her anew. The loss would kill
her. She'd have no one to turn to. CoCo had Luc. Alyssa had
Jackson. Tara wouldn't have anyone to help ease her grief.
She shook her head. No, she wouldn't think along those lines.
She was a LeBlanc, strong and determined.

After passing a broom over the living-room floor and
cleaning the bathroom, she made sure the other two bedrooms
had clean sheets. Then, exhausted, she fell onto her own bed,
staring up at the ceiling fan, whirring slowly, its steady ticking
punctuating the hum of the air conditioner. Her eyelids
drooped.

Bam!

Tara jerked upright, blinking away cobwebs.

Bam! Bam! Bam!

The screen door! Had she even closed it? She flipped her legs over the bed to the floor. "Coming." She stumbled down the stairs, rubbing her face.

"Tara?"

Recognition hit with a slight thrill, followed immediately by irritation. She pushed open the screen. "Sheriff."

"Is everything okay? Are you all right?" His broad shoulders filled the doorway.

A spark of attraction tried to ignite, but she used her annoyance to stamp it out. "Aside from my grandmother being in a coma without any medical reason and you going behind my back to call my family, I'm just hunky-dory. Why do you ask?"

"I'm sorry about that. I didn't mean to cause any problems."

"Yes, indeed." She leaned against the open door. "You accidentally picked up a phone, dialed Jackson's number and informed him that my grandmother's in the hospital? Sure, I can see how that just happens."

"I needed information. You said you were going to notify them. I assumed you'd do that sooner than later."

"Well, you were wrong. Just like you're wrong in thinking what's happening with Grandmere and Tanty is coincidental and random." She ran a hand over her hair, smoothing down the wayward strands. "Was there a particular reason you came by, other than just to annoy me?"

"I was concerned when you missed the last visitation with your grandmother."

Guilt slammed her like a sledgehammer. She cut her gaze to the wall clock. Could that be right? Had she really dozed off for a couple of hours? "Uh, I fell asleep. Has there been a change with Grandmere? I mean, the nurses are supposed to call if there's any—"

"No, no. There's no change. I just got worried about you when you didn't show."

Shame transformed her words into cutting remarks. "I don't need a keeper, thank you very much. I'm a big girl, able to take care of myself."

"I didn't mean to imply otherwise. I on—"

"And I don't need you jumping into my family business." She turned away from the door.

"Look, I said I was sorry about that." He followed her into the kitchen. "Besides, I need to follow up on a couple of things with you."

Standing at the sink, she reached for the sponge. "Such as?" She rested her hand on the hot-water knob.

"You said your grandmother had a visitor before she fell ill."

She glared at him over her shoulder. "And?"

"You said there were dishes left in the sink?" He joined her and jutted his chin toward the plates and cups she'd been about to wash. "Those them?"

She nodded.

He pulled several paper bags from his pocket. "Can I run some tests on them?"

"Please."

He donned latex gloves, then carefully slipped the plates and cups into the bags before shoving the two forks into envelopes. He tossed the gloves in the trash and grabbed his pen. In a neat hand, he labeled the bags, then glanced around the kitchen. "Do you have any idea who might've come to visit your grandmother?"

"I told you, I wasn't here. I haven't a clue."

"Well, these tests will probably net us nothing, but we'll try." He lifted the bags and hesitated. His eyes softened as he stared at her. "I really am sorry. For everything."

The spark flared again. She nodded, sure no words could force their way past the emerging lump in her throat. The door shut softly behind him.

Tara stared out the window, noticing the sun dipping below the trees as the bayou prepared for night. Alyssa and Jackson would be here soon. How could she avoid the confrontation that would certainly take place?

By not being at home when they arrived.

They'd probably stop by the hospital before heading to the house. She could leave them a note, go into work and get the club's books current, take a leave of absence, then go to the hospital for the night visit and slip more of the healing potion into Grandmere. If she played her cards right, she could avoid her sister until the wee hours of the morning. By then, surely Alyssa would be either asleep or too tired to fight.

Yeah, good plan.

Ten minutes and a shower later, Tara dressed and scrawled a note for Alyssa and Jackson. She headed to her car just as an SUV whipped into the driveway. Great. Now what?

An older woman sporting hair an interesting shade of blue jumped from the running board, gripping a casserole dish covered in foil. "Hi, there, honey."

Like she knew this woman? Maybe a friend of Grandmere's? "Hello. Can I help you?"

"I'm from your grandmother's church and brought you this chicken casserole." She reached Tara and handed her the dish. It was still warm. "You can stick it in the fridge if you're on your way out. Easy as pie to reheat. Just put it in the oven at three-seventy-five for thirty minutes and it'll be right as new."

"Thank you." The woman made no attempt to move. "I'm just on my way to work."

"Oh. Don't let me keep you, then, honey. My name's on masking tape on the bottom. Marie will know how to get it back to me." The woman gave a final nod before climbing back into her SUV and backing down the driveway.

Tara ran the casserole into the house, shoved it in the fridge, then headed back out the door. She couldn't risk Alyssa catching her at home. *Mais non.* That wouldn't do. She hopped in her car and sped to the jazz club.

But that casserole had sure smelled good. Her stomach growled as she parked behind the club. When was the last time she'd eaten? She'd grab something on her way to the hospital. In the meantime, she'd snatch all the pretzels she could from the club.

The band neared the end of its last set as Tara wove around people toward the office. She stopped at the bar and smiled at the bartender. "Hey, Mike, can ya give me some pretzels? I'm starved."

He passed her a bag and winked. "Want a cola with that?"

"Please." She turned to face the crowd.

Smoke hung a hazy curtain over the room. The band broke, then left the stage. Voices rose over the jukebox as it kicked on and spewed out old jazz classics. A few couples remained on the dance floor, oblivious to the change in music.

Her boss, Jayden, made his way across the crowded floor and plunked down on the barstool next to her. "Hey, there. I heard about your grandmother. How is she?"

"In a coma. That's part of the reason I came by—I need

to take a leave of absence to be with her. I'll get everything caught up tonight, though."

He touched her arm. "I understand. No problem. I'm so sorry."

"Me, too."

Jayden stood, hesitating. "If you need anything, you just call, okay? I'm here for you."

She smiled as he touched her hand. "Thanks."

He retreated to the back office while she glanced back over the dance floor. Another reason for her to take a leave of absence—Jayden had lately been showing interest in her. Too much interest.

"Hi."

Tara nodded at the woman standing beside her at the bar. Stunningly beautiful, the woman lifted her blond hair off her neck. "It is hot in here, isn't it?"

Something about her accent, along with her striking good looks, struck Tara as familiar. "It's a bit warm, yes." She inspected the woman.

Mike slid a tall cola across the bar to Tara, then widened his smile at the woman. "What can I get ya, honey?"

The woman primped without a mirror. "How about a martini, dry." She flipped her hair over her shoulder and smiled at Tara.

The movement sparked a flash of recognition. It was the woman with the pharmaceutical company's research team. Irritation bloomed in Tara's chest. "I thought y'all would be long gone by now." She took a sip of her drink, watching the woman over the rim of the glass.

"Not until we get what we came for." The comment left no question that the woman knew exactly who Tara was.

"Thought you got it. The other night." Tara set her drink on the bar and clutched the bag of pretzels tighter.

"Not quite." The woman's throaty chuckle changed to a croon as Mike slid a martini glass toward her. "Thank you, so much. I'm downright parched."

Parched? Who used such a word? A Yankee, that's who. Tara lifted her cola and pushed away from the bar. "Just make sure you stay off my land while you're getting whatever else you need. You've been warned."

"Trespassers will be prosecuted?"

Tara narrowed her eyes at the woman's condescending tone, then smiled. "No, trespassers will be shot and fed to the gators."

"Do you have any idea where my sister is?"

Bubba turned from the nurses' station and stared at Alyssa LeBlanc Devereaux. Her husband trailed her, wearing a sheepish look. "I don't know."

Alyssa shook her head. "I can't believe she didn't call me and isn't here now."

"Have you tried her cell phone? I talked to her earlier. She was fine." Bubba shifted his weight from one foot to the other. He'd dropped off the dishes from the LeBlancs' at the lab, grabbed a quick sandwich and headed straight to the hospital, sure he'd see Tara.

He'd been wrong. As he usually was in regard to her. Beautiful, but frustrating.

"I'm sure she is. But she's not *here,* and she's not answering her cell. Someone should be with Grandmere all the time."

Bubba rubbed his chin, dismissing the stubble this time. "We can only go back into the ICU to visit for fifteen minutes every couple of hours. The rest of the time is just hanging out in the waiting room." Boy, no wonder Tara had berated him for calling Alyssa. He'd forgotten how demanding she could be when provoked. He should've remembered. But in his defense, he'd been in ICU himself most of the time she'd been working to find out who attacked him.

A fact he'd never forget.

Jackson lay an arm across his wife's back and extended his free hand to Bubba. "How's your aunt?"

Grabbing his old fraternity brother's palm, Bubba gave a half shrug. "No change." And every hour that passed had him more worried. Neither Aunt Tanty's nor Mrs. LeBlanc's condition had been upgraded from critical, and the fact that the doctors still had no clue what had caused their comatose condition concerned him greatly. Not to mention Tara's admonitions. Or were they accusations?

Jackson smiled at his wife. "Why don't you check with the nurses to see if you can sneak in to see your grandmother while I talk to Bubba for a minute?"

She gave her husband a knowing look, but complied. Jackson moved with Bubba toward a corner in the hall. "Listen, I tried to broach the subject of voodoo with Al, but she went ballistic. I couldn't get anything useful out of her without triggering her curiosity about why I was interested."

Bubba sighed. Just what he'd been afraid of. "I guess I'm on my own here."

"Not necessarily. Al called CoCo and Luc. They're cutting their honeymoon short and catching a flight home tomorrow. If anybody would know about the voodoo stuff, it'd be CoCo."

And she was less of a thorn in Tara's side than Alyssa, that much Bubba knew for certain. "Thanks. I appreciate it."

Jackson glanced over at his wife, who was giving a nurse an earful. "Tell me what you're thinking, pardner."

"When I look at both cases side by side, the only common thing between them that excludes others in town is voodoo."

"What's your gut tell you?"

Bubba pondered that question for a moment. Was he letting Tara's rantings skew his cop instincts? No. The scary part was that his hunch lined right up with her convictions that some person, some outside influence was the cause of what happened to Aunt Tanty and Mrs. LeBlanc.

"I think the voodoo connection is the key to finding out what's going on."

Jackson paused as Alyssa turned from the nurses' station. "Let me see what I can find out. We'll be staying at the house, so I'll nose around a bit."

Eyeing Alyssa's approach, Bubba whispered, "Yeah, good luck with that, Jacks."

"They said I could visit for five minutes, but that's it," Alyssa said. "Better than nothing, I suppose." She smiled at her husband. "But only me. I'll be back in a few." She planted a kiss on his cheek before following a nurse down the hall.

Jackson regarded his old friend. "Why haven't you just asked Tara?"

Bubba almost choked. "Because she barely tolerates me as it is. She wants me to run around and start accusing people. I can't do that." He jutted out his chin. "Haven't you realized your sister-in-law is a bit of a, um, fireball?"

Jackson laughed. "She can be a handful. But she knows voodoo. She trained for a couple of years under her grandmother, and last Al ranted, she'd been visiting your aunt for further instruction." He paused, all traces of laughter gone. "Could Tara be the connection?"

"It's crossed my mind, yes." Bubba had a sinking feeling in his gut. "If she is, she might very well be in danger."

And that was something he couldn't ignore. Not when it seemed she'd slipped under his skin.

* * *

No sign of Alyssa.

Tara breathed a deep sigh and left the elevator. She turned the corner, heading directly to Grandmere's room. Luckily, still no glimpse of her sister. Of course, it being after midnight probably had something to do with it. Just as she'd planned.

She eased open the glass door and slipped into the room. Perching on the edge of Grandmere's bed, Tara withdrew the vial of healing potion. She looked around once, then administered eight drops before putting the vial back in her pocket. She mumbled an incantation and waited.

Grandmere appeared less wan. A hint of pink in her cheeks. Could the potion be working?

The door opened behind her. She jerked to her feet and met the gaze of a nurse.

"You shouldn't be in here now."

"It's my regularly scheduled visiting time." Tara glanced at her watch just to make sure.

"But your sister was here earlier."

Tara crossed her arms over her chest. "And I missed my time before that."

The nurse hitched a brow, a frown creasing her face.

Tara dropped her arms and shoved her hands into her pockets. "It's not like I'm wearing her out any. Please?"

The nurse shook her head. "Sorry, but those are the rules."

"Can't you bend them just a little? Just this once?"

"I'm afraid I can't." The nurse lifted Grandmere's chart. "The ladies from her church are in the waiting room down the hall holding their prayer vigil. Just in case you'd like to join them."

As if. Tara sniffed, dropped a kiss on her grandmother's cheek and headed out the door.

Beeeeeeeeeeep!

Tara shot back into the room just as Grandmere's eyes fluttered.

SIX

As inexplicably as she'd fallen into it, Marie LeBlanc had awakened from her coma. Bubba glanced skyward. The late moon shone brightly on the parking lot. Stars winked back at him. Who knew, maybe Aunt Tanty would wake soon, as well.

Lord, please let it be so.

He crossed the asphalt and strode through the hospital's double doors. His quickening heart set the pace for his steps as he made his way into the elevator and up to the fourth floor.

Jackson, Alyssa and Tara stood in a semicircle in the ICU waiting room when he entered. A group of women from CoCo's church stood holding hands in the corner. Some had tears running down their faces. His friend reached him first. Jacks clapped a hand on his shoulder. "Isn't it a miracle? Reminds me of what happened with you."

Bubba found the words hard to form as memories flooded him. "It is, indeed, a miracle. What happened?" He spoke to Jacks, but his attention focused on Tara.

Her face showed a mix of emotions: excitement and relief with a bit of annoyance added in. Her sister stood beside her, hand on hip. Ah. That explained the annoyance.

"I'd just left her room when the machines let out an awful beep." Tara became animated in the retelling of the event.

Seeing her enthusiasm made Bubba's heart beat a little faster. Man, she was something.

"You were kicked out of her room for visiting outside the proper schedule," Alyssa blurted out, disapproval edging her voice.

"Since when do you care so much about law and order?" Tara rolled her eyes and then met Bubba's gaze. "Anyway, as I was saying, the machine went haywire, so I ran back into the room. The nurse was flustered, pressing buttons and stuff, when Grandmere woke up." Her eyes were like pools of smooth chocolate as her smile flickered into them. His stomach knotted into a tight ball.

"The nurse called the doctor, who's examining her now." She cut her gaze to the hallway. "We should hear something from him any minute. I also asked about Tanty." Tara looked directly at Bubba, her voice softening now. "There's no change."

It didn't make sense. If the two comas were connected, why had Mrs. LeBlanc awakened while his aunt still lay in the coma's dark grasp?

Tara put a hand on his forearm. "I'm so sorry."

That she understood his conflicting emotions and empathized with him meant the world to him, though he wasn't sure why. He'd analyze that later. He coughed to clear his throat. "Once the doctors complete their tests tomorrow, I can ask your grandmother what happened. Maybe we'll get some much-needed answers."

Alyssa clutched Jackson's arm. "At least she woke up. That's got to mean she'll be okay with no permanent damage." She looked at Bubba. "When you were in a coma, the doctors were concerned your vital organs would start shutting down the longer you stayed under."

He knew the drill all too well.

Tara jabbed her sister in the ribs. "*Cooyon!* Tanty's still in a coma."

Clamping her hand over her mouth, Alyssa turned pale and her eyes widened. "I'm so sorry, Sheriff. I didn't think."

"It's okay."

But it wasn't. Tanty had been in a coma longer than Mrs. LeBlanc. She should've been the one to come out first. That would've been right. Fair. Then again, whoever said life was fair?

A doctor appeared in the doorway. "Are y'all Mrs. LeBlanc's family?"

Alyssa and Tara pivoted and answered yes together.

"Preliminary results reflect a positive prognosis for Mrs. LeBlanc. We're still running more tests, but by all indications, the coma caused no lasting damage."

The sisters clung to one another as tears streaked down their faces.

"We're going to remove the machines. We'll continue to run tests throughout the night."

"When can we see her?" Alyssa asked.

The doctor shook his head. "Not for several hours. Five at least." He held up his hand against any protest. "We have to continue these tests to know how to best treat the patient. And she's exhausted, or will be after the battery of tests. She'll need her rest."

"Can't we see her for just a minute?" Tara asked.

Might be none of his business, but Bubba knew exactly, or pretty close, how drained their grandmother felt. "The doctor's right."

Everyone stared at him.

"I remember. It's taxing every time they take you off a

machine. And even though she's been in a coma, she'll just want to sleep." He shrugged. "At least, I did."

The doctor nodded at him gratefully.

"What time do you suggest we return?" Jacks asked the doctor.

"Come around noon. We'll have concluded our tests, and Mrs. LeBlanc will have had some time to rest."

"Noon!" Tara all but stomped her foot.

"Yes, you can have lunch with her then." The doctor was resolute. "You want what's best for her, yes?"

Tara's frustration shone in her glittering eyes, but she bit back any further comment.

Alyssa lay a hand on her sister's shoulder. "Of course. We'll be back at noon." She tugged Tara's arm. "C'mon, we need to let Grandmere's church members know what's going on."

By the look on Tara's face, that option wasn't her top choice, but she let the doctor's dig slide. Bubba walked with the doctor down the hallway. "Doctor, I was wondering if you could give me an update on my aunt, Tanty Shaw."

Bubba glanced over his shoulder at the receding waiting room.

Tara looked right at him, her eyes penetrating. A brief smile played across her lips.

He almost tripped over his boots.

Tara's stomach churned. Bubba Theriot looked so discouraged, so downtrodden over Tanty. It nearly broke her heart.

Wait a minute. Why did she care? He was just a cop, a Jesus follower, someone she'd known practically all her life, but hadn't paid any special attention to. Tall, nicely built, with red hair—and his gait showed a slight limp every now and again. Bubba wasn't anyone to get excited about. Was he?

So why did her stomach feel funny every time she got around him lately? Probably just nerves. A lot had happened in a short time. Nothing to get excited about.

"Coming?" Alyssa asked. The ladies from the church had disbanded, going home to call the other members of the congregation to share the good news. They truly thought their prayers had been answered, that God had healed Grandmere. Their conviction touched Tara, but it didn't make sense. Not to someone who understood the truth. Yet they believed *so much*. So strongly.

Tara shoved her hands into her pockets. Her fingers touched the vial. Her heart sped. The healing potion! That was what had brought Grandmere out of a coma. It worked, no matter that everyone else believed in a miracle from heaven.

She needed to get it into Tanty. Fast.

"Uh, I'm gonna go check on Tanty for a minute."

Her brother-in-law hitched a brow. "Isn't Bubba with her? They won't let you in."

"I know. But since Grandmere's doing so much better, maybe—"

Alyssa threaded her arm through Tara's. "Come on, you're not gonna sneak in on Grandmere and get in trouble with the doctors again."

Resentment stuck in Tara's craw, but she allowed herself to be led into the elevator, out of the hospital and across the parking lot. Better to pick her battles carefully.

The breeze had picked up, stirring the dust. The sky hung clear over their heads—no sign of rain. If Lagniappe didn't get something soon, all the plant life would die.

Foliage!

She'd have to gather from the bayou when she got home if she planned on visiting with Grandmere at lunch tomorrow.

Most people didn't feel safe in the swamp after dark, but Tara'd grown up playing in it. Besides, she had her voodoo to guide and keep her safe, yes?

She followed the taillights of her sister and brother-in-law's car down the winding road home. Maybe they'd go to bed as soon as they got home, allowing her to sneak into the bayou without having to explain. Yet another argument with Alyssa just wasn't on her agenda. Not at three in the morning.

After parking, the trio trekked up the wooden stairs to the LeBlanc plantation home. Jacks opened the door. Alyssa crossed the threshold. Tara hesitated. Jacks quirked a single brow. "Coming?"

She took a deep breath and lifted a casual shoulder. "I think I'm going to sit out here for a while." She flashed him a half smile. "I have a lot to process."

He stared at her for what felt like an eternity, then nodded. "I understand. I'll be praying for you."

Every muscle in her body tensed. Praying. Yeah, that worked so well. Had the entire town become delusional? Sure seemed that way with all the talk of praying and miracles. But she didn't have time to argue the point. She turned and faced the bayou, letting the smell of water and moss wash over her. The door creaked behind her before a soft catch sounded.

She waited a few minutes, then rushed to the workhouse. She grabbed her collection bag in the dark, not chancing that Jacks or Alyssa might glance out the window and catch her. Slipping the strap over her shoulder, Tara shoved her feet into the rubber boots by the door, grabbed a flashlight and then headed toward the deep part of the bayou.

Dry grass and dead leaves crunched under her boots and the beam of her flashlight bounced as she made her way farther into the wooded bowels of the bayou. A hoot owl sounded, followed by a gentle stir of wings as it took flight. Tree frogs cried for rain. She could relate.

Tara inspected several plants, all dry and withering. She'd have to get closer to the bayou canal to find viable foliage for her potions. Adjusting her route, she headed toward the water's bank.

The moon reflected off the still bayou. A sheet of glass was what it looked like. Tara bent to inspect the plants near the edge of the water, kneeling on the mushy ground.

Crackling footsteps reverberated through the dense underbrush. Tara turned off the flashlight and glanced up, her gaze sweeping the area. Something big rustled behind her, making the hair on the back of her neck jump to attention. A figure in black ran past, heading in the direction of the main outlet to open waters.

What in the world…?

Tara jumped to her feet, heart thudding. Her fingers dug into the worn canvas of her satchel.

The revving of a boat engine carried over the still bayou. Tara dropped her collection bag and ran all-out toward the inlet. Her thigh muscles burned as she jumped over fallen logs and ducked under low-lying branches. Adrenaline pushed her harder, faster.

She reached the clearing at the inlet's mouth just in time to catch sight of a boat exiting the canal and turning into the main waterway. Squinting, she could make out nothing identifiable about the craft. She fought to catch her breath, bending at the waist and planting her palms on her knees.

Who'd been running through the bayou in the wee hours of the morning? More importantly, why?

The peace of the bayou was lost for her now. Violated. Tara meandered back through the woods, collected her stuff and trudged home, her heart heavier than the empty bag. Gathering potion ingredients would be futile when she was in this mood. One thing Grandmere had taught her well—when selecting ingredients, your mind must be on visualizing the potions you're collecting for. Otherwise, there was the chance the potion wouldn't work.

She entered the shed and flipped on the light. It hardly mattered if her sister saw the light now. More than likely, Alyssa was sound asleep, cuddled up next to her husband. Loneliness washed over Tara in waves. Tears burned her eyes. For a moment, she saw Bubba and how lonely he had looked, too, standing with the doctor and worrying about his aunt.

No. She wouldn't go down that road again. She'd made her choice, and it was to pursue her training over a relationship. Blinking, she focused on the room—and let out a startled cry.

The room sat in utter chaos. Papers were tossed all over the workstations and floor. Broken glass littered the tabletops. Leaves and stems were scattered everywhere. The window was shattered. Chairs and stools overturned. Shelves ajar, their contents broken and lying in heaps.

Fresh tears stung. Only this time, they were tears of frustration. Anger.

Who would do such a thing? Tara's gaze darted to her sister's bedroom window. No, not even Alyssa would go this far, no matter how much she detested Tara's involvement with voodoo. Tara pressed her palm against the bridge of her nose.

The person running through the bayou. Running away. From what he'd done. Him. Yes, with her eyes closed, Tara could make out the blurred figure. Well over her five-six. Wide shoulders. Definitely a man. What else could she recall? He'd been wearing all black. If only she'd thought to turn her flashlight back on. Had he even known she was there?

Which made the next question storm Tara's mind—what had he been doing here? Obviously looking for something, but what? There was no other logical reason, given the state of the room. He had to have been looking for something specific. What?

Grandmere never kept detailed records like Tanty. Maybe this person didn't know that. Had he been a client? Someone with an ax to grind? No, this didn't look like petty vandalism. This looked like more of a search. On top of Tanty and Grandmere both falling into comas so suspiciously, this felt ominous. Sinister.

Tanty's!

If this was connected to the illness somehow, then it stood to reason that Tanty's shed would be next. Already she'd found things out of order at Tanty's, just not trashed like this. Would the intruder be back?

Tara ran to the kitchen door, snatched her keys from the hook and jumped into her car. Her fingers fumbled getting the key into the ignition. She turned the engine over and tore out of the driveway. Gravel and dirt rose in a cloud over the vehicle as she sped down the road toward Tanty's.

The sky shifted from night to predawn. Purple hues streaked the sky to the east. Tara's heart pounded as she turned into Tanty's driveway.

Lights blazed inside the workhouse.

Slamming on the brakes, Tara jerked the car into park, raced to the workhouse—and then stopped dead in her tracks.

Bubba Theriot opened the door and stepped outside, gun drawn, his glare intense. He stopped advancing as he caught sight of Tara and holstered his firearm. "What're you doing here?"

She popped her hands on her hips. "What're *you* doing here?"

He glanced down. Spook meandered between his legs and meowed. He locked his stare back on Tara. "Feeding the cat. Now your turn—what're you doing here?"

"Uh, well, I, um…" Her throat constricted.

Narrowing his eyes, he took her by the elbow. "I told you to stay away from here. I'll ask one more time—what're you doing here?"

How dare he manhandle her? She jerked free of his grip and glowered. "I just found my shed trashed, and I thought maybe Tanty's had been, as well."

"When?" He withdrew his ever-present notebook and pencil from his front pocket.

"Not even thirty minutes ago. And I saw him."

"Who?"

"The guy who did it."

He sighed. "Who was it?"

"I didn't see his face."

Bubba's expression fell. "Then how do you kn—"

She let out a huff. "I was in the bayou and heard someone running. He raced right behind me on his way to his boat. I chased, but he was too far ahead of me by the time I caught up. I couldn't make out anything about the boat, either."

"How does this have anything to do with your place being trashed?"

"As soon as the boat was out of sight, I went back to my shed and found it trashed. Like someone was searching for something."

"So, you really don't know that the person running through the bayou is the same one who went through your place?"

Could he be any more dense? "Why else would a person be in the bayou at three in the morning?"

"*You* were."

Touché. Oh, good-looking or not, the man infuriated her. "I was on my own property. He wasn't."

"You're sure it was a man?"

She went through as much as she recalled, her toe tapping against the ground.

"What made you think my aunt's place had been rifled through?"

"Well, let's see. Your aunt goes into a coma, followed by my grandmother, and we still haven't a clue why. My grandmother was a voodoo priestess, your aunt is one." She shrugged. "Stands to reason if my place was searched, someone would search Tanty's. Remember, they didn't fall ill by themselves."

"And you have proof of this?"

Why wouldn't he just listen to her? "Yes."

His brows shot into his forehead. "You do? What?"

"I already told you. I felt it."

"Right. Voodoo. How silly of me to forget." He closed his notebook sharply.

Tara's irritation rose even further. "I realize you'd rather believe in the religious fantasy than the truth, but there's no need for you to be so rude about it."

He shook his head. "I'll follow you to your place and check it out. File a report."

She locked her eyes on his. "Why won't you believe me?"

"Because I deal in law. Rules. Proof. Evidence. Call me crazy, but I need concrete things like that to solve a case."

"Then how come you have *faith* in Jesus? Don't you have to have faith to be a Christian?" Tara spun on her heel and got back into her car. "Of course you do. But you'll regret you didn't have faith in *me* when I prove I'm right." She glanced over her shoulder and caught him staring after her. "Yeah, proving you wrong will be sweet."

She revved the engine. Heading down the winding road home, she spied his headlights in her rearview mirror.

"I think it will be *very* sweet."

And as much as the man annoyed her, what bothered her more was accepting the fact that she was attracted to him.

SEVEN

Tara LeBlanc had to be the most frustrating woman on the planet. As he finished up in the work shed, Bubba completed his notes for his report, stuck the digital camera back in the truck's console and stared at her. Studied her. Took notice of her gestures and body language. Some women bit their nails when nervous, but not Tara. Nope, she flipped that long hair of hers over her shoulder when she became agitated. And talked more with her hands.

Right now she spoke with sarcasm lacing each word she forced out. "I would ask you in for a cup of coffee, but I don't want to wake Alyssa and Jackson."

Something about the way she hesitated caught him off guard. "Have you checked on them since you found this?" He gestured toward the mess.

Her tanned face paled. "I didn't check the house."

He nodded. "Let's go check it together."

"I can do it." She flew to the kitchen door like water raging over a dam. He shook his head and followed. He was running into this woman too much lately. Frankly, it wasn't good for his nervous system. He wasn't sure why, but somehow Tara LeBlanc had worked her way under his skin.

Wait just a minute! She was only CoCo's little sister, Jacks and Luc's sister-in-law, right? Nothing more. So why did his pulse race whenever she got near him? He shook his head again. He must be tired. Really tired.

She glanced into the kitchen. "Looks fine. I'll just tiptoe upstairs and take a quick look-see."

He felt certain everything was fine in the house, but needed to check. "I'll go look around your shed."

He made his way to the side of the shed facing the bayou, shining the flashlight over the wall, roof and ground. Even though dawn had nearly broken through the dusk, artificial light would be the only way to detect a clue. If they could spot one. He didn't hold out any expectations of finding anything.

The light reflected off something on the ground behind a wilted hydrangea bush pressed close to the building. Bubba donned a pair of latex gloves and gently pushed the limp leaves aside. A brown bottle lay nestled against the bottom of the bush. He took the bottle and read the label in the flashlight's beam.

Purple Haze beer by Abita Brewing Company.

He set down the flashlight and withdrew an evidence bag from his pocket. He slipped the bottle inside and sealed the envelope just as Tara joined him.

"What's that?" She nodded to the envelope.

"You drink Purple Haze?"

"What? Are you kidding? I don't drink."

"Really?" That was interesting.

"Really. Why, do I look like a lush?"

"Uh, no." Great. Open mouth, insert size twelve shoe. He should know better.

"Oh, I see. Because I'm not some religious freak, I must

be a drunk." There she went with the hair flipping. "Well, I'm not. Did that whole drinking gig back in high school. Haven't touched the stuff since."

Oh, yeah, he remembered. Tara pulled a couple of stunts attributed to underage drinking. He'd been called out to "talk" to her once. She'd been just as enraged then as she was now. How could he have forgotten that?

"Did you find it out here?"

He jerked his attention back to the present. "Yeah. Under your hydrangea. Know anyone around here who drinks Purple Haze?"

"Not that I can think of. Do you think *he* left it here?" She glanced around the area behind her. "Kind of an odd place to drop a beer bottle, don't you think?" She faced him and the shed adjacent to them. A large window stood only inches above the top of her head. Her eyes widened.

"We don't know who it belongs to. Let's not panic."

She shook her head. "No. Wait. He couldn't have stood out here watching me because we'd just gotten home. I only grabbed my bag and boots before I headed into the bayou. Didn't even turn the lights on inside."

"I told you not to panic. I'll just see if we can pull a print off the bottle. We'll see what comes up."

"But…"

"What?"

"What if he'd been watching me before?" She spoke more to herself than to him. "What if he saw me with the paperwork and didn't know I'd taken it into the house? What if that's what he was looking for?"

"Tara?"

She jerked her gaze to his.

"What're you talking about? What paperwork?"

Even in the rising sun's dim light, he could see her cheeks turning pink. "Uh, just some work papers."

"For the jazz club?" Now they might be getting somewhere. If she brought home some accounting paperwork...

"No. Personal."

"But you said work stuff."

She cocked her head. "Voodoo stuff, if you must know."

He should've guessed. But something about her flaming face hit him funny. "What kind of paperwork?"

"Client details and stuff." She squared her shoulders and huffed. So much for her being uncomfortable with his line of questioning. "Things you wouldn't be even slightly interested in."

"If it pertains to this case, then I'm interested." He retrieved his flashlight and shone the light around the ground next to the bush.

"Thought you didn't believe this *was* a case. You said there was no evidence of any foul play with Tanty or Grandmere."

He snapped his glance to her. "I'm referring to *this* case. Here and now." He looked at the ground around the bushes. Wait a second, was that a footprint in the ground next to the wall? Bending, he shone the light to the area right under the eaves. Sure enough, there was an imprint of what appeared to be a boot in the softer ground. He straightened and faced Tara. "Do you water around here?" The bushes sure didn't look like she did, but the ground right next to the shed was softer, damp.

"I dump my excess liquid out the window." She gave a sheepish shrug. "I like to think it makes up for not watering the plants as often as I should. Why?"

He couldn't swallow back the smile. "Looks like it's paid off. I found a footprint next to the bush."

She took a step forward. He grabbed her elbow as gently

as possible, remembering how she had pulled away the last time he'd tried to touch her. He softly tugged her back. "I need to photograph it."

"Oh."

He passed her the flashlight. "Hold this and stay put. I'll grab my digital and be right back."

All but sprinting to his truck, he retrieved his camera and hurried back to Tara. She hadn't moved an inch, thank goodness. He carefully pushed aside the bushes and aimed the lens. "Can you shine the flashlight over my shoulder, please?"

He felt more than saw or heard her move closer. Her intoxicating perfume filled the air with a fresh spicy smell. The urge to take her in his arms rose. He shook off the thought and focused the camera. Just take the pictures. Gather the evidence and get out.

Click. Click.

He turned the camera and bent, taking pictures at different angles. Five, six more. His finger froze before he pushed it a seventh time. This was ridiculous. *He* was ridiculous. Taking more pictures than necessary, just so he could keep Tara close. Stupid.

Straightening, he studied the print.

"What do you think?"

"Ah…" He rubbed a hand along the back of his neck. "Looks to be about a size eleven or twelve. Steel-toed."

"How can you tell?"

He bent and pointed around the toe of the print. "See how this is a bit wider and deeper? Means it was heavier. Most people don't walk on their toes. But steel toes mean more pressure at the top."

She nodded and smiled. Was that admiration glistening in her eyes?

He needed to snap out of this crazy thinking. Taking the flashlight, he surveyed the surrounding ground. Not a single other print. "When was the last time you tossed something out this window?"

"Hmm." She tapped a finger against her chin. "Last night when I finished brewing the heal—"

He hitched a brow when she didn't finish.

"Last night. I mean, the night before Grandmere woke up. Came out of a coma. Whatever."

What had she been brewing in her little shed? Something she didn't want to share with the class, that much was certain. "So, whoever stepped here had to have done so within the past twenty-four hours."

"I'd think so."

He made a final notation in his notebook and glanced toward the house. A single light burned in the kitchen. "I'm assuming Jacks and Alyssa were fine."

"They're still asleep." She brushed her hands over her shorts. "I don't want to wake them. They're exhausted."

And Alyssa would probably still give Tara an earful. He couldn't blame Tara for trying to avoid that. "Well, I'll file my report and see what the lab can come up with on the bottle and footprint."

She walked him to his truck. "I appreciate it, Sheriff."

"You can call me Bubba, you know." He hadn't the first clue why those words had jumped out of his mouth. He certainly hadn't intended to say such a thing.

She smiled. "I think I'd rather call you Sheriff." She turned and took two steps toward the house before glancing back over her shoulder. "Or René." She winked before opening the door and sliding inside.

He froze. Her soft chuckle drifted to him on the morning breeze. What was he getting himself into? *Lord, give me wisdom here.*

Godly Women.

Morning sunlight peeked around the curtain, filling the kitchen with light as Tara rubbed the edge of the business card. She couldn't stop wondering if Suzie was connected to this whole thing. She wanted to call and ask her, but what would she say? Maybe it was a crazy idea born of no sleep because of the events of the night before. And why on earth had she winked at Bubba, actually winked at him?

Back to Suzie and the business card. Alyssa and Jackson were at the airport picking up CoCo and Luc, so they weren't around to ask any questions. But how could she broach the subject with Suzie?

She could just call this number for Godly Women and thank them for the meals, yes? Ask to speak to Suzie, since she gave Tara the card? She'd just be extending good southern manners.

Tara headed upstairs to her bedroom, still gripping the card. She picked up the phone and pressed the numbers.

One ring.

Even her sisters couldn't fault her for this fishing expedition. Just being polite.

Two rings.

Okay, so she still had no clue what she'd say if Suzie actually answered. "Hey, did you ever try to get Tanty Shaw to handle a private female problem for you and then poison her and my grandmother?" just wouldn't be polite.

Three rings.

What was she doing calling? She had no business contacting Suzie. It probably wasn't even the same woman from Tanty's client list.

"Hello." The female voice came out breathy. "Godly Women."

Tara's hand clutched the receiver.

"Hello?" the voice said again.

"Uh. Suzie?"

"Yes, this is Suzie. Who's this?"

Her greatest hope and biggest nightmare, all rolled into one. "This is Tara LeBlanc."

Silence.

"Marie LeBlanc's granddaughter."

"Oh, yes. We heard the news about Marie. It's a miracle from God."

Yeah. Sure. Right. "It's great news."

"Is there something specific we can pray for you, Tara?"

Please, no. "Actually, I wanted to thank you for the casserole y'all sent over. It was delicious." How lame could she sound?

"You're most welcome. We'll be bringing more over this evening, as well. I understand your sisters and brothers-in-law are now staying with you?"

News traveled fast in such a small community. "Yes, they'll all be here tonight."

"We'll make sure to bring two casseroles. I know how men eat." Suzie's laugh rang false in Tara's ear.

This could be perfect. "Will you be delivering them?" Tara held her breath.

"I don't think so. I believe Evelyn is assigned supper tonight."

So much for wishful thinking. "Oh. I'd really like to talk to you a bit, if I may."

All traces of laughter fell from Suzie's voice. "About what?"

Think fast, Tara. "Um, the church. Grandmere."

A pregnant pause hung over the line.

Finally Suzie sighed. "I suppose I could visit you at the hospital this afternoon. I'm scheduled to be in the prayer session there from one until three."

"Perfect. I'll find you. Y'all will be in the waiting room, yes?"

"Uh, I believe so."

"I look forward to seeing you then." Tara replaced the receiver before Suzie could change her mind. And it sure sounded like she wanted to.

But why? It'd been Tara's experience that if the door to a religious conversation opened, most Christians leaped over the threshold. Sure enough worked that way with CoCo, Alyssa and Grandmere. Yet Suzie certainly didn't sound excited about sharing the Jesus message with her. Odd.

Tara raced down the stairs and out the door. The work-house still stood in total disarray. She'd have to clean it up later this afternoon. But not now. She needed to get the healing potion. Today she'd get some of the potion into Tanty. Her heart raced. Today could be the day that Tanty came out of a coma.

She grabbed the small vial, shoved it into her jeans pocket, then bolted to her car. Her game plan was all laid out—slip in and give Tanty the potion, check on Grandmere, then meet with Suzie to try to find out what was going on.

The hospital's elevator felt stuffy, confined. Tara touched the vial in her pocket to calm herself. She had to get her mind on the healing chant. Focus. Concentrate.

Edging into Tanty's room, Tara glanced around. Luck was

again with her, as no one hovered nearby to observe. She slipped the dropper from the vial and administered the last two drops on Tanty's tongue. She'd have to make more. Closing her eyes, Tara chanted quietly.

"Aren't you up and about early?"

Tara jumped from the side of the bed and pivoted. Bubba stood in the doorway, arms crossed but wearing a welcoming smile. She flashed a nervous smile in return. "I just wanted to check on her before seeing Grandmere."

"I appreciate that. It's nice of you." His voice was husky, clogged with emotion.

She pushed the vial deeper into her pocket. "Well, I'd better go."

His broad shoulders blocked the entire doorway. His gaze caressed her face in a way that made heat rise to her cheeks. He put his strong hand on her shoulder. "I feel I ought to warn you."

Taking a step back, she quirked a brow. "About?"

"Alyssa's back here with CoCo."

EIGHT

There wasn't supposed to be a complication. Tara stared at the doctor.

"She's still conscious, but we're having to keep her on strong medication for the pain, which makes her sleep."

"I don't understand. She wasn't in pain when she came out of the coma yesterday," Alyssa said.

The doctor nodded. "I know. But something began making her violently ill a few hours after we'd begun testing."

"Could the tests have made her sick?" Tara just couldn't grasp how Grandmere had been fine yesterday and now lay comatose again.

"Not likely." The doctor gave one of those condescending smiles they must teach in medical school. "It could be a residual side effect from whatever made her sick to begin with."

The person who poisoned her had struck again. Tara shoved down the rage coursing through her veins.

"Can we at least sit with her?" CoCo snuggled under Luc's arm.

He hesitated a moment. "For a little bit. Just two at a time and only for fifteen minutes. I'll tell the nurses to adjust the visiting schedule every hour, so you'll get fifteen minutes."

Alyssa nudged CoCo. "You and Luc go in. We got to see her yesterday."

CoCo shot a questioning glance at Tara. "Okay?"

Tara nodded. She really wanted to see Grandmere, but knew CoCo did, too. Besides, she'd go hunt down Suzie and see if her last name was Richard. And she had "news" she could pass on to the little group. Give 'em something to pray about.

Avoiding Alyssa, Tara strode down the hall to the waiting room. Sure enough, eight women sat in chairs pulled into a circle. They all looked up as Tara marched in.

Suzie was on her feet first, despite her pudgy middle. "How's Marie?"

"Not as well as we'd thought."

The older woman who'd brought the casserole placed a warm hand on Tara's forearm. "What's wrong, hon?"

Tara explained briefly about the pain and what the doctor had told them.

The woman patted Tara's arm. "Don't you worry none, hon. We'll be lifting prayers for her right now." She eyed the others in the group. "Right, ladies?"

Murmurs of agreement went around the circle. As the ladies joined hands, claustrophobia jabbed at Tara. She motioned Suzie toward the door. "Can we talk outside maybe?"

Suzie followed Tara down the hall and into the elevator. "I shouldn't be gone too long. We want to really pray for Marie's complete healing."

Whatever. "This shouldn't take too long. I just wanted to touch base with you about a few things."

The elevator's dinging prevented Suzie from answering. She trailed Tara across the foyer and out the front doors of the hospital.

Tara chose a secluded bench for them to sit on and began. "I'm sorry, with everything going on, my manners have slipped. I don't remember your last name."

Suzie smiled and sat. "Oh, I understand. It's Richard."

Heart skipping, Tara struggled to keep her excitement in check. Richard was a common surname in south Louisiana. "That sounds so familiar to me. Maybe Grandmere mentioned it sometime?"

"Could be. My husband is a deacon in the church."

Ah. Now that was interesting—her husband a deacon and she visiting a voodoo priestess. *If* she was the same Suzie Richard. "I have a strange question for you."

Suzie stiffened. "About?"

Now would be the time she'd appreciate a little tact and diplomacy like Luc's younger sister, Felicia, possessed. Tara swallowed and wet her lips. "I'm sure Grandmere shared with you her old ways."

Suzie cocked her head.

"The voodoo."

With wide eyes, Suzie nodded. "Yes, she did share her testimony how God delivered her from such evil."

Tara resisted the urge to set the poor woman straight. She took a deep breath. "Yes. I'm sure she also shared with you that I believe in the spirit world."

Suzie hitched her brows. "Well, yes, she did." She leaned closer to Tara and lowered her voice. "We're praying for you daily."

Ignoring that statement, Tara continued, "She probably mentioned I'm still in training in my field. Now under Tanty Shaw's tutelage."

Suzie's face paled rapidly. Ah, this *was* the Suzie Richard who'd visited Tanty. Now, how best to proceed…

"Uh, I don't think I knew that." The poor woman ran a hand over her stomach.

Tara felt a cold chill. Were the spirits trying to tell her something? She needed to pay attention, notice every detail. She took a moment to consider every nuance of Suzie's every expression, movement, gesture. "Well, I am. I'm sure you're aware that Tanty was hospitalized recently. She dropped into a coma just like my grandmother."

"I…I had heard that, yes." She wrung her hands.

"Well, I went by to feed her cat, and several of Tanty's client records were out of place."

Although Tara hadn't thought it possible, Suzie's color drained even more. Too late. She'd come this far, she had to take it to home plate. "I found one on a Suzie Richard, dated just last month."

Suzie's hand flew to her mouth, and her eyes filled with tears.

Tara's heart ached. While she'd still get to the bottom of the story, this poor woman couldn't have had anything to do with harming Tanty or Grandmere.

So why were the spirits still giving her the chills?

"I…I…You can't tell anybody I went to see Ms. Shaw. Please." Fearful tears filled her eyes.

Tara shook her head. "I won't. But it looks odd, doesn't it? You go to see her for something a month ago, she denies your request, then she lapses into an unexplained coma. To top it off, it's not like Tanty to have papers misfiled. Yet, there were three misfiled." She squeezed Suzie's knee. "Surely you can see how odd it looks, yes?"

Suzie's shoulders shook with sobs. "Did it s-say why—" she sniffed and hiccuped "—what I saw her for?"

Moment of truth. "No. Just that it was a female issue and that she referred you to a physician."

Pressing her lips together, Suzie nodded but offered no further explanation.

"Can you tell me what you went to see Tanty for?" Nothing like pushing on.

Fresh sobs racked the woman's body. She fought to stand. "I c-can't. My h-husband…well, he'd be f-f-furious." Suzie looked at Tara with a frightened gaze, pressing her hand to her tummy. "I'm sorry. I can't help you." She got up quickly, took several steps toward the hospital doors, then stopped and faced Tara. "Please don't talk about this to anyone. Please."

"What do you mean there's no match?" Bubba glared at his deputy over his coffee mug.

Gary Anderson handed the report across the desk. "Just that. We were able to lift prints from the cups taken from the LeBlanc home and from the beer bottle you found on the property. We eliminated Marie LeBlanc's prints from one of the cups. The FBI's report on the print from the other cup is a no-match."

"So we have no idea who was at Mrs. LeBlanc's the morning she fell into a coma." Bubba raked a hand through his hair. Could the news be more frustrating? He had nothing to investigate.

"We're sending the feds the print off the beer bottle. Maybe that'll give us a lead."

"Do the prints from the cup match the ones from the bottle?" He needed a break in this case.

"Not that we can tell." Anderson shifted his weight from one foot to the other. "But we're not trained in this kind of stuff, Sheriff."

"I know that." He let out a long sigh. Snapping at his deputy wouldn't help. Anderson didn't deserve such treatment. Bubba controlled his tone. "Maybe they'll be able to find a match for that print. I wish the parish would give us more funding to have all the computer equipment we needed. Then we wouldn't have to wait so long for results."

"I sent the prints express, so maybe the results will come quicker."

"Good thinking." Bubba tossed the report on the desk. "Anything else in here I should know about?"

"The tox results."

"The what?" Bubba reached for the papers and thumbed through them.

"You'd asked the lab to run tests on the residue inside the cups. The report came back as inconclusive."

He didn't bother to ask as his gaze lit on the report in question. Scanning the preliminary results, he stopped at the actual findings.

RESIDUAL FINDINGS: TRACE COMPONENTS FOUND INSIDE CUP. COFFEE DETECTED ALONG WITH SUGAR AND CREAM. UNIDENTIFIED COMPONENT WITH TRACES OF PARALDEHYDE. ADDITIONAL TESTING ON THIS COMPONENT NEEDS APPROVAL.

He glanced at his deputy. "Have we granted approval for this additional testing?"

"You have to authorize that, Sheriff."

Frustration built behind the acid burning his throat. "Fine. I authorize. Call the lab, fax them, whatever we need to do to get them to figure out what that unidentified component is."

"Yes, sir." Anderson spun on his heel and charged from the room. A man with a mission.

Bubba shook his head and stared at the report. Paraldehyde. What was that? He laid the papers on his desk and rubbed the back of his neck. He'd never heard of such a word, and he'd been trained in various street drugs and their scientific names. Whatever-hyde didn't ring any bells.

Unless it was something Tara used in her voodoo stuff. An herb, maybe? Like those swamp plants his aunt was always out digging up?

He needed to find out.

Lifting the receiver, Bubba flipped open his notebook and retrieved Tara's cell phone number. Maybe he'd catch her in a good mood.

"Hello."

Didn't exactly sound like she was in the best mood. Never the mind, he had a case to work.

"Tara? Sheriff Theriot here."

"What can I help you with?"

"I need to ask you about the cups I took from your sink," he said.

"Yes?"

Oh, how could he word this without angering her? She already sounded a bit on the testy side. "Well, the initial lab results have come back."

"And? Did you find something?"

"They've found traces of coffee, sugar, milk and—"

"Grandmere drinks more of a café au lait than coffee."

"Yes, well…"

She wasn't going to make this any easier on him.

"Just spit it out, Sheriff. What else?"

"Traces of an unknown chemical."

He could make out her quick intake of air, even over the bad reception of the cell phone. "I knew it."

Knew what? "Tara, did you put any herbs or anything in y'alls coffee? Even for medicinal purposes?" *Please say no.*

"What?" Indignation filled her voice. "You think I poisoned my grandmother? Are you daft, Sheriff?"

"I didn't mean intentionally. And there's no proof that what they found is what caused her illness."

"Don't be stupid. I didn't put anything in the coffee—never have. I wasn't even home then. Plus, Grandmere trained me, and we never mixed potions with ordinary substances. Tanty's the same way."

At the mention of his aunt's name in relation to potions, Bubba's stomach twisted. "I didn't know. I had to ask."

"Are you having tests run to find out what it is?" Accusation dripped over the connection.

"Of course." Great, now he'd made her mad. He could just picture her, too, flipping her hair over her shoulder, eyes shimmering with flames. A spicy one, for sure, she could be as hot as the cayenne pepper that liberally laced most Cajun dishes.

"Good. Glad to hear you're at least following up."

He let the dig slide. He'd just insulted her in an offhand, unintentional manner. "I just wanted to check with you."

"Well, you have."

Although her tone was bitter, and slightly rude, he remembered she was hurting. And he didn't want to get off the phone with her yet, no matter how illogical his budding attraction was. "We found a print on the cup, as well as one on the beer bottle."

"And?"

Just as snappy as ever. "We've ruled out one set of prints as they're your grandmother's."

"It is her house, you know."

He chose to let that one slide, too. "A different one popped up on the cup. We sent it to the FBI to run through their database. No results matched."

"Wait a minute. The FBI's database couldn't find a match?"

"No." He waited for the tirade to come. Even braced himself by pressing his back deep into the chair.

A long pause and then, "So whoever visited Grandmere and poisoned her doesn't have a criminal record."

"We don't know she was poisoned, Tara."

"I do. I've known someone was responsible. You just haven't gotten enough *concrete evidence* to convince yourself. Meanwhile, my grandmother's sick and your aunt's still in a coma. Why don't you wake up and face the fact that someone's behind this?"

He wanted to, desperately, but there were no facts to support such a claim. Yet.

"Now you've found traces of something unknown that she drank. How much more *concrete* do you need? But instead of investigating that angle and trying to find out who visited my grandmother that morning, you'd rather call me and in-sinuate I had something to do with her getting sick."

"I never said you had any—"

"I'm not finished, Sheriff. Have you sent the report to the hospital to have them run tests on Grandmere and Tanty to see if any of this unknown stuff is in their systems? Have you ordered further testing to identify what it is?" She murmured under her breath, her words unidentifiable to him, but the tone clear. Mad as a gator stuck in a trap.

"Tara, we're looking at every piec—"

"Why don't you just out-and-out accuse me, Sheriff? I am

the voodoo woman, remember? Much easier just to blame me rather than actually having to work a case, yes?" Her words tumbled over each other. "Well, I'm not to blame and if you can't figure that out, then you're more of a *cooyon* than I thought!"

He opened his mouth to interrupt just as a click sounded. Was her cell cutting out? Four seconds later, another click. She'd hung up on him!

He could almost understand. She felt as if he'd accused her of harming two of the people closest to her. He didn't believe she'd do that for even a minute.

But his training whispered in his ear. Sometimes the guilty went on the offense to throw the scent off them. No, that couldn't apply to Tara LeBlanc.

Could it?

NINE

The gumption of the man! All but accusing her of poisoning Grandmere. Sheriff René "Bubba" Theriot had really pushed her to the limit this time. Why did the man continue to get under her skin?

Tara shoved the broom in the closet and surveyed the workhouse. It'd taken a couple of hours and lots of elbow grease, but the room was now back in order. She let out a slow breath. Released the anger. Drew in the fresh air. She had to get her anger under control or she couldn't gather plants, and she really needed to make another healing potion for Tanty. One dose hadn't done the trick with Grandmere, and Tanty'd been in a coma longer. She'd probably require at least three.

Continuing to take deep cleansing breaths, Tara hummed a Cajun tune. If only CoCo and Luc weren't still at the hospital, Luc could play his sax for her. Zydeco music always lifted her mood. For now she'd just have to make do with humming.

The adrenaline at last subsided, she grabbed her bag and slipped her feet into the rubber boots, then took off for the water's edge deep in the woods. Cicadas cried in the afternoon heat. Birds rustled the dry leaves of the trees. An isolated breeze stirred the Spanish moss hanging from the cypress trees. Lagniappe was in for a long hot summer.

Tara quickly gathered foliage, filling her bag to overflowing, and returned to the shed. She pulled off the boots and wiggled her toes. Footwear was a necessary evil, in her humble opinion. If given the choice, she'd be barefoot forever.

The cuckoo clock announced two o'clock. Tara burst into action. Having set up a rotating schedule with her sisters for visiting Grandmere, her time would be at three. She selected the freshest plants she'd picked and lit the burner. Her back ached as she concentrated on mixing just the right amount of ingredients in the glass flask. Sweat glued her shirt to her back. At last, the potion was ready to place on the burner. Very carefully, Tara put the flask atop the burner and adjusted the open flame. Her chant came as a whisper, then grew louder as bubbles burst forth in the potion.

She lowered the heat and continued to chant. This part of the process was critical. Every word had to be said with confidence. Each bubble of the boil had to be gentle so as not to burn, yet forceful enough to blend all the ingredients.

Finally the potion was complete. Using pot holders, Tara poured the mixture through a colander, gathering the liquid in a small glass vial. She straightened and twisted the dropper-top on tightly.

"A healing potion?"

Tara jumped and turned.

CoCo stood in the doorway, her arms crossed over her chest.

Shoving the vial into her pocket, Tara shrugged. "How'd you know?"

CoCo laughed. "I trained for more years than you, *Boo*. Do you think I wouldn't recognize the chant?" She moved across the room and looked at the damp solids in the colander.

Leave it to her sister to remind her that she was Grandmere's second choice in training a replacement. "But I thought once you were a Christian you forgot all this stuff."

"Becoming a Christian didn't erase my memory, Tara, only my sins."

Whatever. "Well, I guess I'd better be getting up to the hospital. You know how Alyssa will gripe if I'm late."

CoCo laid a gentle hand on Tara's shoulder. "You know *your* sins can be erased, as well, right?"

A lump the size of a lily pad filled her throat. Tara swallowed, pushing it back down. "I'm fine."

CoCo's eyes were soft. "Deep inside, you know I'm telling you the truth. I've never lied to you, nor will I start now."

The words wouldn't come, nor would the sarcasm she relied on so often when someone pressed her back against a wall.

"That potion isn't the answer." CoCo gestured around the room. "None of this is. But there is a definite answer. Positive. Full of hope and life. Promises."

Tara's eyes stung. The fumes from the burner must be getting to her.

CoCo enclosed her in a hug, then tightened the embrace. "God loves you, Tara. He's waiting for you to accept Him and His free gift."

Tara jerked away from her sister and pawed at her eyes. "Don't try to fill my head with that nonsense. You've already brainwashed Grandmere and look where that's gotten her."

"Oh, *Boo*, you can't think that."

"Then explain to me how your precious God can let this happen to her. She bought into the whole Jesus tale. What has that gotten her?"

CoCo took a step toward her. "Eternal salvation, that's what accepting Jesus has gotten her." She reached for Tara, only for Tara to take another step backward. "We can't always understand why things happen, but we need to accept that God's master plan is what's best for us. You can have the peace and salvation, too."

Why did she even bother to stand and listen to such nonsense? "No, thank you. I deal with the cold hard truth. I can see potions working, touch the plant life I work with, feel the earth under my nails. What can you feel with your God?"

"The wind blowing. The clouds rumbling."

"That's nature, not God."

"He created it all, *Boo*."

"Yeah, well, he can create me gone. I'm heading to the hospital." Tara grabbed her keys and shoved her feet into the clogs by the door. "Lock up for me, will ya?"

She made it into her Mustang and down the driveway before her tears spilled. What was wrong with her? Crying because her sister had become delusional? No, it couldn't be something so silly.

Bubba.

That's what had gotten her emotions all out of whack. Him accusing her, casting shadows on her voodoo abilities. Making her feel less confident. It was all his fault.

She whipped into the hospital parking lot and stomped inside. After checking her watch and noticing she had a few minutes until she could see Grandmere, Tara slipped three doors down and stuck her head in Tanty's room. There was no one with her. Tara crept inside, withdrawing the vial from her pocket as she looked around.

She administered four drops of the potion to Tanty, planted a kiss on her cheek, and then exited the room just as the doctor rounded the corner of the hall. She made a beeline for him. "Doctor?"

He stopped, squinting. Probably trying to place her. "Yes?"

"I'm Tara LeBlanc, Marie LeBlanc's granddaughter."

"Oh. Yes. How can I help you? I'm afraid there's no change in your grandmother's condition."

Big surprise. "Has the sheriff contacted you in regards to running tests on my grandmother and his aunt, Tanty Shaw, to look for a particular, undefined substance?"

His brows furrowed. "No. But it'd be hard to test for something undefined. Why would we do such a thing? Exhaustive bloodwork on both patients has turned up nothing out of the ordinary."

"You wouldn't know unless you looked for it, right?"

"I'm not following, young lady."

Tara swallowed back an exasperated sigh. "If you could be told to look for something in particular, even if it was unidentified, could you find it?"

The doctor shoved his glasses back to the bridge of his nose. "Perhaps. Although we'd have to know at least a partial component."

"Such as chemical traces of paraldehyde?" a deep voice asked.

Tara spun to face the sheriff. Her back stiffened. "It's not nice to eavesdrop."

He ignored her and continued to address the doctor. "Could you run tests on the patients and see if there are any traces of paraldehyde?"

The doctor rubbed knuckles over his chin. "We could. But why?"

"I want that test run on my grandmother." Tara shoved her way between the doctor and the sheriff. "Immediately."

Bubba continued as if she hadn't spoken, "Would paraldehyde show up in any of the tests you've already run?"

Tara bit back the sharp retort she had ready to blast at the sheriff. She wanted to hear the doctor's reply more than she wanted to get back at Bubba.

"No. The tests we've run wouldn't have detected any paraldehyde. We'd have to order a special test."

"I want that test on my grandmother." Tara raised her voice. Both men shifted their focus to her.

Finally.

"I want you to administer the test to my grandmother."

"Well—" the doctor began.

"No. I'm her next of kin and am requesting the test. No, I'm *ordering* the test." She popped her hands on her hips. "Do I need to sign a permission form or something?"

"I suppose I can order the test, but I don't see much point in it."

Tara rose to her full height. "I don't care what you see, Doctor. I want that test given to my grandmother. Now."

The doctor's face flushed, and his glasses slid to the bump on his nose. "I'll draw up the paperwork now."

"Merci."

The doctor turned and strode down the hall to the nurses' station. Game, set and match to the little people. Victory made her lips curve into a smile.

"What're you trying to prove?"

"I'm trying to prove my grandmother was poisoned by whomever visited her that morning." Tara jabbed a finger in his direction. "And you should have Tanty tested for it, as well."

"There's no evidence of my aunt having been poisoned. Your grandmother, either, for that matter."

She let out a groan that could only be described as coming straight from her gut. Flames shot from her eyes, and she flipped her hair over her shoulder. "Aside from them both just falling into a coma for no reason, that para-hyde stuff being found in Grandmere's cup and them both involved in voodoo, you mean?" She rubbed her hands over the sides of her jeans. "Come on, man, open your eyes."

He had to admit when all the circumstantial evidence was laid out like that, it pointed to there being someone behind the women's illnesses. But circumstantial evidence wasn't enough. He needed more. The law required it.

"Look, if your grandmother's test comes back positive for traces of paraldehyde, then I'll have Aunt Tanty tested."

"And waste precious time?" The muscles in her jaw jumped.

His tolerance held. Barely. Like he wasn't doing all he could to figure out what was wrong with his aunt, why she was still in a coma. "Look, that's really none of your concern."

She pressed her lips together as if holding in her opinion. Wouldn't that be a first?

"Look, I know you're only trying to help because you care about my aunt, but I have to treat her case and your grandmother's as totally different. There's nothing to imply foul play in my aunt's case."

Again her jaw muscles twitched.

He rested his hands on the Sam Browne belt around his hips and lowered his voice. "I have to do what I think is best, Tara."

She paused and then nodded. "What is that para-hyde stuff, anyway?"

He motioned her toward the waiting room. "From what the lab techs told me, it's used as a sedative or hypnotic."

"What?"

"It was first used back in the late 1800s. However, because

its toxicity level is five, other medications have replaced what it originally was used to treat."

She dropped into one of the plastic chairs. "What are the side effects?"

He sat beside her. "They can range from respiratory problems to…" He gripped the arms of the chair.

"To coma, right?"

At least she didn't have a snide tone. He nodded.

"How fast does it work?"

"They tell me it's immediate."

She sucked in air. "Is it available on the market today?"

"Not readily. From what I've been told, it's been replaced with less-dangerous drugs." He leaned back. "But keep in mind it wasn't actually paraldehyde that was found in the cup. It was a chemical trace of it."

"Which means?"

"It's something akin to probably a synthetic of the main component of paraldehyde, but not the full drug itself."

Her brows knitted. "So, it's sort of a hybrid of the original?"

He nodded again, not sure what else he could say. He, too, had been stunned after his phone conversation with the lab technician.

"Who would be able to do that? Change the chemical makeup, I mean."

"I don't know."

"Maybe that's where we should focus our investigation."

We. He liked that she chose that word. Had a nice ring to it. Wait! He needed to snap out of such fantasies.

"What about the print on the beer bottle?"

"We've sent it to the FBI. It'll take some time to get their results."

"In this day and age, you'd think it'd be immediate."

He chuckled. "Not in Lagniappe. We're lucky we even have a fax machine and an old computer. Not that it does us much good—we keep getting knocked offline."

"Don't tell me the sheriff's office is still on dial-up."

"Yep. We don't have funding to upgrade yet."

"That stinks."

"Yeah, it does. But we sent the print express, so hopefully we'll hear something within a week."

She smiled at him. His stomach tightened again. What was going on with him?

"Hey, Tara." A tall man approached, wearing a smile and carrying a cup of coffee bearing the local diner's logo.

"Why, hello, Jayden. What're you doing here?" Tara's entire face lit up as she smiled.

"Heard your grandmother's improved and wanted to stop by and say hello." He handed her the cup. "I would've brought flowers, but know they don't allow them in the ICU."

Bubba cleared his throat, discomfort seeping into his every pore.

Tara glanced at him, then darted her gaze back to the man who stared at Tara as though she was the light of the universe. "Sheriff Theriot, this is my boss, Jayden."

Bubba shook the man's hand because Southern manners dictated he do so. But his heart twisted inside. Was this also Tara's boyfriend? He hadn't heard anything about Tara being involved with anyone, but as beautiful as she was, it wasn't a stretch of the imagination that she'd be taken.

No, that couldn't be right. That had to be the ugly green-eyed monster filling Bubba's head. Tara had introduced Jayden as her boss, not her boyfriend. And if she had a boyfriend, surely he would've been with her through all this ordeal.

For some reason, that made Bubba very glad. And he immediately chastised himself. He had no business in Tara's personal life.

After a few more polite exchanges, Jayden left. Despite himself, Bubba was glad the man was gone.

Tara took a sip from the cup and fell right back into their conversation. "I don't think the person who trashed my workhouse is the same one who poisoned Grandmere."

"Why do you say that?"

"Because I didn't get that feeling."

Voodoo again. His spirits sank. "Oh." He fought to find a decent response, one that wouldn't raise her hackles.

A nurse approached. "Ms. LeBlanc? You can go back to see your grandmother now."

Tara thanked her and stood. "I appreciate you sharing this with me, Sheriff."

He stood and smiled until he noticed her expression change. He followed her line of vision to the hall.

A woman in scrubs grabbed a chart and headed away. He glanced back to Tara, who was looking intently at the retreating woman. "What's wrong?"

"That woman…" She kept staring at where the woman had been standing. "I thought I recognized her."

He touched her shoulder until she looked at him. "You've probably seen her around here while visiting your grandmother or my aunt."

"Maybe." But her eyes darted back to the hall.

"Well, you should head on back. Maybe your grandmother will be awake."

Tara jerked her gaze back to him and snorted. "Not likely. I haven't a clue what pain med they're giving her, but it sure keeps her zonked out."

"You don't want her in pain."

"No, but I don't want her to stay in a drug-induced coma, either. If she were awake and coherent, we could just ask her who'd visited her."

As if he wasn't praying for Mrs. LeBlanc to be conscious enough to share that information. Who she identified could blow the whole lid off his investigation. "I know. And she will, as soon as they can find why she's in so much pain."

"Probably that para-stuff. Does it cause pain?"

"The tech didn't mention that, but I'll call him back and ask as soon as I finish visiting Aunt Tanty."

She grabbed his hand and startled, seeming to feel the same connection he did. Then she looked at him pleadingly. "Please consider having Tanty tested. I know it's all related. You just have to trust me." She smiled and then was gone.

Trust her? The woman he'd grown to care about but who cared more about voodoo than Jesus? He needed to trust God. But running the test on Tanty couldn't hurt.

He walked to the nurses' station to request the test.

TEN

Did it have to be so unbearably hot?

The afternoon sun beat down on Tara's car as she drove to the Carlson residence. Yeah, she'd be stepping out of line by showing up at their home, but she needed to talk to Rebekah. The woman's reaction to what Tara had to say would make it clear whether she was a suspect in what happened to Grandmere and Tanty. It'd certainly make Tara scratch Suzie Richard off the list.

Suzie's reaction left no doubt in Tara's mind that she was too timid to do something as outlandish as poison two women. Although connected to both, Suzie had been too fearful of her husband finding out. Did that give her more motive? Tara shook her head. No, every bit of her voodoo training led her to the fact that Suzie hadn't been involved in Grandmere's and Tanty's illnesses.

If only the sheriff would listen to her and do what he should—investigate. But no, he couldn't do that. Too simple and logical. Stubborn man. If he'd take her seriously, she could tell him about those three client sheets, then he'd have a starting point for the investigation. Instead, he had dismissed her allegations. Well, she'd find the answers, the truth, even if he was too pigheaded to do it himself.

Flipping on the turn signal, Tara moved to turn into the Carlson's driveway, only to have to slam on her brakes. A white SUV careened from the drive, a man behind the wheel who didn't look too happy. But he did look familiar. But from where? As he passed, she caught a better look at his face. That man from the pharmaceutical company! What could he be doing at Mayor Carlson's?

She turned into the Carlsons' driveway and parked behind a Mercedes. Nice car. She glanced at the house. Correction, nice spread. Big white columns lined the front veranda. Red brick circular driveway. Ferns and airplane plants in baskets draped between the columns. Very sweet.

Her steps were cautious as she made her way up the concrete stairs. She hadn't even raised her hand to grasp the knocker when the door swung open. Rebekah Carlson stood there.

Tara stepped back, her heart hammering.

"I'm sorry. Didn't mean to startle you."

"Just caught me off guard." Tara gave a little laugh and mentally berated herself. What? Did she think she lived in some true crime novel now?

"What brings you by?"

Tara noticed she hadn't been invited inside, as Southern manners usually dictated. Interesting. She shucked off the little voice in her head questioning her ability—her right, even—to do this and forged ahead. "I'm sure you heard about my grandmother and Tanty Shaw."

Rebekah's eyes softened. "I did. We're so sorry and are praying they both have full recoveries."

Hmm. Maybe. Maybe not. "Yeah. Well, because I've been

working with Tanty, I've noticed some paperwork misfiled in her office. Certain client information, to be specific." She arched a single brow and waited.

Four seconds lapsed before Rebekah's eyes widened, and she sucked in a quick breath.

Bingo! Tara nodded. "Yes, one of them was yours. About visiting Tanty regarding your husband's, uh, condition."

Horror marched across the woman's face as she glanced down the driveway. "Why don't you come in?"

Tara stepped into the foyer. The marble floor hadn't a single blemish. Crown molding lined the top of the wall to the ceiling.

Rebekah shut the door, but remained standing. "I…I don't know what to say." She put her trembling hand against her throat. "Is that information out in the open? I mean, does anyone else know about this?"

"As far as I know, no."

"But?"

"But someone had been rifling through Tanty's records and yours was misfiled. I can only assume someone was looking for something in particular. I don't know who, if anyone, actually saw the notes on you."

Rebekah shook her head and clasped her hands in front of her. "I was desperate, you understand. My husband wouldn't see a doctor. I needed help from somewhere."

"I know. Trust me, I understand. And I'm discreet. I'm in this business, remember?"

"I never went back after someone saw me leaving. It was horrible." Her gaze darted out the window toward the road.

She was clearly hoping no one saw them talking, yet didn't invite Tara to sit down or somesuch. Something was odd here. "Did the potion work?"

"Oh, yes. Wonderfully." Rebekah smiled.

"That's great. But you didn't go back?"

The smile froze on her face. "No. That Melvin Dubois saw me leaving and mentioned it to my husband. My husband said it didn't look good for the mayor's wife to be seen with a voodoo priestess, that people would talk." Her voice dropped with each word until she barely whispered.

Melvin Dubois. Another one of the client sheets misfiled. Coincidence? "And that's what made you stop going?"

"My husband was furious." She glanced out the window again. "Still is. He has people watching me to make sure I don't go back." She swallowed loudly.

Ah, now they were getting somewhere. "Would he have been angry enough to go through the papers in Tanty's work-house?"

Rebekah tossed an icy glare at her. "Now if he'd gone rummaging through someone's things, don't you think he would've taken them and not left them for you to find misfiled?"

Score one for Rebekah Carlson.

Rebekah stood straighter. "Besides, my husband's the *mayor*. He doesn't go around poking through other people's belongings."

But would he be desperate enough to take Tanty and Grandmere out of the picture so they couldn't talk? Maybe he'd hired someone to find the paperwork, and they'd failed.

"I think you'd better leave now." Rebekah opened the door and backed away.

"Mrs. Carlson, one more thing."

"What?" Exasperation flashed in her eyes.

"Does your husband still suffer from his, uh, condition?"

Rebekah narrowed her eyes. "That's none of your business." She pushed open the door wider. "And I'd advise you not to discuss this with anyone."

Tara paused on the veranda, facing Rebekah. "Is that a threat, Mrs. Carlson?"

"Oh, no, my dear. That's just a bit of friendly advice. My husband's a powerful man, you know."

Bolting down the stairs and to her car, Tara turned on the ignition and let the air conditioner blast against her face. She sat still, thinking.

Mayor Carlson might be powerful, but he was impotent.

Would that information be enough to cause him to take drastic measures to keep his secret?

She didn't know, but she sure-as-shootin' aimed to find out. Soon. Tara glanced at her watch—thirty minutes until her visit with Grandmere. She had time to drive over to City Hall and see what Mayor Carlson had to say. Better reach him before Rebekah did. Well, she'd probably already called him. Tara recalled the mortification on Mrs. Carlson's face. No, she wouldn't call him. Maybe she would tell him when he got home, if at all. It wasn't exactly polite dinner conversation. *Oh by the way, honey, I discussed your little problem with Tara LeBlanc this afternoon. Would you please pass the salt?*

A car screeched around her in the driveway, yanking Tara from her imagined scenario. Lo and behold, Mr. Mayor himself got out of his little convertible. Tara killed the engine of her car and got out. "Hello, Mr. Carlson."

His face held the practiced smile of a politician. "Good afternoon. May I help you?"

Her sweaty palms had nothing to do with the relentless heat. "I'd actually dropped by to talk to your wife, but what I had to say also applies to you."

He stopped at the trunk of his car. "And you are?"

"Tara LeBlanc."

Recognition lit his eyes. "Marie LeBlanc's granddaughter? The one doing that voodoo nonsense?"

She was really getting tired of everyone knocking her way of life. "Yes, and yes."

"What could you possibly have to say that applies to me?"

"Why would a pharmaceutical research team leader be visiting your home?"

"Not that it's any of your business, but it's my job as mayor to try and bring industry and commerce into the area."

"By destroying our bayous?"

"Young lady, I believe you've outstayed your welcome. Is there anything else?"

His arrogance grated on her nerves. "What about why your wife went to see Tanty Shaw?" She crossed her arms over her chest.

His face turned different shades of red. His brows lowered into a straight line, and he shook like a dead leaf in the breeze. "Get off my property, young lady. Leave now, and never come back."

Now *that* was a reaction. "But, Mayor—"

"I said get off my property." His tone didn't imply he was in the mood for polite conversation.

Tara rushed to her car, twisted the key, then whipped around the circular driveway to the main road. Her heart pounded.

Innocent or not, Mayor Carlson had just jumped to the top of her suspect list.

"…badgering my wife and me. Me, the mayor."

Bubba moved the phone back to his ear. Mayor Carlson's yelling had nearly broken his eardrum. "I understand, sir, and will get right on it."

"Tonight, Sheriff. I will not tolerate disrespect from such a person."

Such a person? She'd love that. Oh, well, he had a job to do. "Yes, sir. I'm leaving right now."

He replaced the phone and shook his head.

Tara, Tara. Did she even realize the can of worms she'd opened?

He grabbed his radio and shoved it into his belt. Glancing at the clock as he stood, he figured Tara would be at the hospital with her grandmother. She couldn't answer her cell phone inside, so he might as well drive over. He was torn with mixed emotions—anticipation at seeing her again and dread at the confrontation he would face.

Lord, give me the words.

The interior of the hospital felt cold to his sweat-dampened skin as he made his way up to the fourth floor. Sure enough, upon exiting the elevator, he spied Tara leaning against the wall outside the waiting room. He approached her with his heart in his shoes. "Don't feel like sitting inside?"

She smiled. "Grandmere's church group is in there praying. I don't think I'd be too welcome."

"You might be surprised."

"I'd rather not be." Her smile widened.

He hated having to jump in and ruin the peace between them, but duty called. "Speaking of surprises, I just had one."

"Really? Do tell."

"I just received a call from Mayor Carlson." He paused, giving her the opportunity—no, mentally begging her to apologize and promise she'd stay away from the mayor and his wife.

She said nothing. Just crossed her arms over her chest and jutted out her chin.

"Care to tell me why you accosted him and his wife on their property?"

"I didn't accost anyone."

"Then what would you call it?"

"I had a few questions to ask, that's all."

"That's all?" He raked his hand over his hair. "What kind of questions?"

She grinned like she'd just won the Louisiana Lottery. "Didn't the mayor tell you?"

"No, he didn't. Why don't *you* tell me?"

She chuckled and shook her head. "How can he accuse me of accosting him if he didn't tell you what I asked?"

"Drop the coy act. Just tell me."

Her facial muscles stiffened. "It was private."

"Apparently. Enough that the mayor called me in an outrage. Demanded I order you to stay off his property and away from him and his wife."

"How convenient."

This was getting him nowhere. "Look, just tell me what's going on. Can't you see I'm trying to help you here?"

"Help me?" She pushed off from the wall and stepped into his personal space. "If you want to help me, why aren't you out there trying to find out who poisoned my grandmother? That'd be a help, instead of me trying to do it on my own."

Ah. That was what this was about. No wonder the mayor was livid; he detested those who practiced voodoo. "What did you do, Tara?"

"I merely told him something I know."

"Which was?"

"Private, like I said."

"Look. Something caused him to call me and yell for over fifteen minutes in my ear. What did you say?"

"Well, I have reason to suspect the mayor might have been involved with what happened to Grandmere and your aunt."

"Based on what? Your voodoo again?"

"If you don't want to hear the answer, don't ask the question, Sheriff." She turned and took a step.

Bubba grabbed her arm and pulled her back to him. He tugged a little too hard, and she landed against his chest. The fresh scent of her perfume, or maybe it was shampoo, swarmed his senses, intoxicating him. He dropped her arm and stood staring at her, fighting to regulate his breathing. She'd never looked so beautiful before.

How could this young woman he'd known for years suddenly cause such a response in him?

She glared into his face and stepped backward. "Don't touch me again," she ground out from between clenched teeth. "Ever."

"I'm sorry. I'm just trying to—"

"Help. So you've said."

"Why don't you believe me?"

"Why won't you believe *me?*" She crossed her arms again. Impasse.

"Ms. LeBlanc? You may see your grandmother now."

Tara nodded at the nurse, but didn't break eye contact with him. "Is there anything else, Sheriff?"

Something about the challenge in her eyes undid him.

"Yes." He pulled her to him again. "Come here. I *am* going to touch you again, but only to give you a hug. You've been all alone in this until your sisters showed up, and I know this is hard. I do want to find out what happened to Aunt Tanty and your grandmother. No, we *will* find out what happened to them." He pulled Tara to his chest and held her gently. Tara went stiff for a fraction of a second, then relaxed against him.

As quickly as he'd charged, he retreated. She wobbled in his embrace. He steadied her. "You'd better go see your grandmother."

For once, Tara LeBlanc was speechless. She gave a curt nod before marching down the hall.

What was wrong with him? What had he done? He was supposed to warn her to stay away from the mayor, not hold her in his arms and make promises he didn't know how to keep.

But how his heart had pounded as he'd held her.

He was so in a world of hurt.

ELEVEN

Sooner or later, something had to give.

At least, that was the philosophy Tara held to at the moment. She pulled two more leaves from the stem and ground them in the stone mortar with the pestle. Daylight quickly faded into night, streaks of purple decorating the skyline over the trees. If she planned to finish preserving the foliage before it got too late, she'd better get to crackin'.

And what about the sheriff's embrace? What was up with *that?*

She ground the leaves almost to liquid and then froze. If she didn't pay better attention, she'd ruin the stock. With the droughtlike weather, she couldn't afford to waste a single leaf or stem. She'd have to keep her wits about her. Now wasn't the time to ponder Bubba Theriot's motives or actions.

Even if his hug had felt like coming home.

Tara slammed the pestle onto the table, her hands trembling. What was happening to her? A simple hug from a man she didn't particularly like right now reduced her to a simpering mess. She shook her head. No. She'd deal with figuring out her emotions later. Right now, she had to concentrate on making the healing potion and figuring out who did this to Grandmere and Tanty.

Suzie Richard's face flashed across her mind as fast as a hurricane making landfall. Tara's hands stilled. Suzie. She'd acted so strangely. Why was she frightened her husband might find out she'd visited Tanty?

If only Tanty had written what, exactly, Suzie had consulted with her about, maybe then Tara could figure out why the woman kept coming to mind.

Every instinct in Tara told her that Suzie wasn't involved in the attacks on Grandmere and Tanty, yet she lingered in Tara's thoughts. Why?

She ground carefully as she went back over every little detail, every movement and nuance of Suzie. Aside from being embarrassed and frightened her husband would find out, nothing else about the woman stuck out.

Tara clenched her teeth. What was she missing?

"What're you doing?"

Tara jerked around to face Alyssa. "Just grinding some foliage." What would possess her sister to step foot inside what she'd dubbed a *heathen haven?*

Wrinkling her nose, Alyssa entered cautiously. "Oh." Her eyes widened as she gazed about.

"Don't worry. No head of bat or eye of newt today."

Alyssa's cheeks filled with air, then she exhaled slowly. "Ha. Ha." With a hand pressed to her stomach, she ventured a little farther into the room.

What, no sarcasm from the queen? Tara narrowed her eyes and studied her sister. Alyssa's color was wan, yet there was a distinct glow about her. A freshness to her skin. Her eyes blinked, the irises sharper, clearer. Even the scar under her lip took on a refreshing radiance. And her hair…it shone under the fluorescent lighting, full of luster and body. Something different, yet not…not sick. Something…

"I wanted to talk to you for a minute." Even Alyssa's voice came out softer. She leaned her hip against the table.

Tara knew in that moment what was different about her sister.

Smiling, she hugged Alyssa. "You're pregnant!"

Alyssa put her hand on her stomach and gave a little gasp. "How'd you know?"

"I just do." She squeezed her sister again. "When are you due? How long have you known?"

Alyssa laughed. "We found out right before we came. Doctor says I'm due early February."

Tara laid her hand on her sister's stomach and smiled. "Healthy. Do you want to know if it's a girl or boy?"

"We haven't decided yet, but we have time. The doctor says we won't have the ultrasound that can tell the baby's gender for a couple of months. We'll decide later if we want to know."

Tara grinned and hugged her sister again. "Congratulations. I'm so happy for you."

"You're gonna be an aunt."

"That's so amazing."

"I know." Alyssa worried her scar with her finger.

Uh-oh, a sure sign she was nervous. Tara took a step back. "Is something wrong?"

"I, well, I just wanted to let you know Jacks and I have decided to name CoCo and Luc the baby's godparents."

CoCo. Not her.

Because CoCo had Luc and are together, they could be godparents? Alyssa would have to find some single guy to be the godfather if she chose Tara as godmother.

She looked back at Alyssa.

No. That wasn't it.

"Look, Jackson and I talked a long time about this."

"Hey, it's your baby. Do what you want." But pain squeezed Tara's heart in a viselike grip.

"You aren't a Christian, Tara."

"Bet that made your choice easy, yes?" She turned back to the pestle and mortar. "No skin off my back."

Alyssa laid a hand on Tara's shoulder. "It's not like that."

Tara shrugged off her touch. "It's not? Oh, I see. This way of life was okay for Grandmere for years. CoCo, too, until she gave it all up for Luc. But because I hold true to the traditions, I'm not good enough to be your baby's godmother." She blinked back the tears she refused to let fall in front of her sister. "I don't care. It's silly, anyway."

"I don't want to hurt you."

Glaring, Tara met her sister's gaze. "I'm not hurt. Because you don't want me to be godmother? That word is offensive to me, anyway."

"I see." Alyssa swallowed and licked her lips. "Okay, then. I guess that's all I needed to say."

Tara nodded. "Congratulations again. Tell Jackson I'm happy for you both."

"All right." Alyssa paused. "CoCo left supper on the stove before she left." She waited a moment. When Tara didn't answer, she turned and exited as quietly as she'd entered.

Tara gripped the edges of the table, digging her nails into the worn wood. What was with her lately? Her emotions had become so tangled. Totally unlike her. First Grandmere. Then the sheriff. Now Alyssa. What would stir up her heart next?

She loosened her grip and rested her elbows on the table, cradling her head in her hands. There was something else niggling her. An impression. Some little thing she should be catching. What?

Again her conversation with Suzie flashed through her mind.

The woman's wobbling. Her sobs. Her pleading not to share the information with anyone. Her tears and hiccups.

Wait! Tara pinched her eyes closed.

Suzie's hand on her stomach. Just like Alyssa.

Suzie was pregnant!

Tara struggled to recall Tanty's notes exactly.

Female issue. Recommended to a doctor. Suzie didn't want her husband to know. She became distraught. The medical procedure didn't allow for total discretion. Had Suzie become pregnant and wanted an abortion? Nah, couldn't be. No voodoo priestess would perform such a procedure. Besides, Suzie was married. Didn't married couples want kids? Wait a minute!

Straightening, Tara opened her eyes. Could it be that Suzie had seen Tanty for infertility problems? That would fit, for sure. Especially if she did end up going to a fertility specialist without her husband's knowledge and got pregnant. She sure wouldn't want him to find out, and Tanty would be considered a loose end.

But how did Grandmere fit into the picture?

Maybe Suzie had approached Grandmere before Tanty. No, the time frame didn't match.

But Grandmere joined the church Suzie attended. The one where her husband was a deacon.

Could Suzie have been afraid Grandmere knew of her visit to Tanty and would say something? That'd be strong motivation to silence both Grandmere and Tanty.

Tara stored her stock and washed the pestle and mortar on autopilot, her mind flipping through the possibilities. The healing potion would be ready tomorrow, and she'd make sure Tanty got a full dose.

Whatever happened with Grandmere and Tanty, Suzie Richard was back on the list of suspects.

Just seeing Tara sent ripples of warmth through him. This had to stop.

He'd managed to avoid her in the ICU halls, darting into Aunt Tanty's room when Tara passed. Childish? Perhaps. But he didn't know how to deal with what he was feeling. And he certainly didn't want to discuss why he'd embraced her.

Or how the embrace had affected him. Next time he might be tempted to kiss her.

His life would be so much simpler if he wasn't starting to care about Tara LeBlanc so much. Yep, he'd acted on feelings he'd been experiencing for several days. Days? Had it only been days? Felt like years.

Lord, what's going on with me? Why now? Why her? *She doesn't love You. What do I do?*

He let the bushes outside the hospital door shield him as she approached. He definitely didn't want to run into her out here, where there were no other people. She'd have him at her mercy. He ducked his head as she passed.

She marched toward the parking lot aglow with security lights. He was about to head back to the hospital entrance when something flashed in the lot. Just a flicker of light from the old pickup truck parked a row behind her car.

He inched free of the bushes and obtained a clearer view.

Car lights on, Tara pulled slowly from the parking space. She headed toward the exit.

The truck's lights popped on, and the engine rattled to life. It followed Tara's car at a distance of about two car lengths.

Coincidence? Or was someone deliberately following Tara? With all that had been happening lately he couldn't chance it.

Bubba sprinted across the lot and into his truck. He quickly caught up to the pickup and reached for his radio. After calling in the license-plate number, he kept the pickup and Tara's car in his line of sight while he waited for the dispatcher, Missy, to give him the report.

Three right turns and the pickup continued to follow Tara. Now he knew beyond a shadow of a doubt that she had a tail.

The radio crackled. "Sheriff?"

"Go ahead, Missy."

"Truck is registered to a Melvin Dubois. Need the address?"

"No. Can you check and see if there are any warrants out on Mr. Dubois?"

"Sure thing. Hang on."

Static filled the cabin of his truck. A left turn, followed by a right. The pickup still kept a safe distance behind Tara, but was definitely following her. Every so often it'd veer toward the shoulder, only to jerk back onto the pavement.

The radio crackled again. "Sheriff?"

"Go ahead, Missy."

"Nothing outstanding."

"Priors?"

"Two DUIs and one public disturbance."

"How long ago?"

"Last DUI was three months ago. Public disturbance back in October."

"Thanks."

"Sheriff?"

"Yes?"

"Need me to send Deputy Anderson your way?"

Bubba glanced at the pickup still tailing Tara. History of DUIs and public disturbance, not a good mixture. Six more miles and she'd be on the deserted road leading to her house. "Yeah." He gave Missy his location and direction, then slowed his truck. No sense giving away his presence until backup arrived.

"Any specific instructions, Sheriff?"

"Radio position every five minutes and wait for my directive."

"Ten-four. Base out."

He took the turn onto the deserted road almost at a crawl. With no streetlights lining the road, his headlights would give away his cover if the driver of the pickup happened to look in his rearview. The taillights from Tara's car glowed in the distance as she took a curve.

He couldn't see the truck. Where was it?

Police instinct pushed Bubba's foot harder on the gas pedal. He still couldn't see the truck. There were no turnoffs on this part of the road. It couldn't have just disappeared.

Then he saw it. A flash of reflection off her taillights as it gained on her. The pickup had its lights off. It would ram into her car any minute now.

So much for waiting for backup. Bubba flipped on his light and activated the siren. The bayou erupted with the wails.

Tara's brake lights came on, then were darkened by the pickup as it crashed into the back of her car.

The radio in Bubba's truck squealed to life. Anderson radioed his location, only three or so miles from the turnoff. The sheriff informed him of the situation, then signed off.

In seconds he skidded to a stop behind the pickup and Tara. They'd stopped in the middle of the road. Bubba exited the car, his hand on the grip of his Beretta.

Correction, *Tara* had stopped. The pickup's grill was imbedded in her bumper, rendering it unable to move. Wasn't from lack of trying, however. The man behind the wheel gunned the engine. The pickup jerked, but the bumper held tight.

Tara stood outside the driver's door. "Are you nuts?"

"Get to the other side of the road. Deputy Anderson will be here in a moment," Bubba told her.

Once satisfied that she did as instructed without argument, Bubba drew his gun and pointed it at the driver. "Sir, please turn off the truck and exit slowly. Keep your hands where I can see them."

A long moment passed. A million scenarios played out in Bubba's mind. He'd only drawn his firearm a handful of times in the line of duty and had never shot anyone. Would tonight be the night that would all change?

Another siren wailed in the distance. Deputy Anderson, right on schedule.

In the dark, Bubba couldn't make out the driver or what he was doing. "Sir, I said turn off the engine and exit slowly, keeping your hands where I can see them." He kept the man in his sights.

The engine died with a cough. The driver's door opened with a creak. Bubba kept his weapon aimed.

A large man dropped his foot to the pavement. He heaved the rest of his massive bulk from the vehicle, keeping his hands in plain view.

"Step from behind the door and move to the site of impact. Place your palms on the trunk of the car." Bubba never wavered in his aim.

"What's this about, Sheriff? I ain't done nothing wrong."

"Just do as I say, sir."

The man swayed as he followed Bubba's instructions. Once his palms were on the trunk, Bubba patted him down.

Not detecting any weapons, he holstered his sidearm and withdrew the handcuffs. He cuffed the man just as Deputy Anderson pulled up. Stepping from the cruiser, Anderson drew his weapon.

Tara, never one to take orders well, crossed the road. "What kind of moron rear-ends someone?"

Bubba shot her a glare. "Be quiet." He nodded to Anderson. "Take her to your cruiser and get her report of the accident."

"Accident?" Tara exclaimed. "He rammed into me. Didn't even have his headlights on."

"Enough, Tara." He lowered his voice. "Just go with Deputy Anderson."

While his deputy escorted Tara to his cruiser, Bubba turned the driver of the pickup to face him. "Do you have a license on you?"

"In my wallet. Back left pocket."

Bubba reached around and withdrew the worn nylon wallet.

"Why'd you cuff me over an accident?"

Bubba eyed the license. "Mr. Dubois, I've been tailing y'all since you left the hospital, and you were following Ms. LeBlanc. I have every reason to believe you rammed her car intentionally." He reached for his small flashlight.

"What? I did not."

"Where're you headed, Mr. Dubois?"

"Uh, I'm going froggin'. On the bayou."

"What part of the bayou?"

"Fisherman's Cove."

"Uh-huh." He shone his flashlight into the man's face. "Mind if I take a look in your truck?"

When Dubois nodded, Bubba inspected the bed of the

truck. Nothing back there but empty beer bottles. He pulled his baton from his belt and nudged the bottle until it rolled. The label shimmered under the flashlight's beam.

Purple Haze.

Bubba checked the cabin of the pickup, then faced the man. "Mr. Dubois, there's nothing in this truck to indicate you were going froggin'. Why don't you just tell me why you were following Ms. LeBlanc?"

"I know my rights. I don't have to answer any of your questions." He shifted until he leaned on his cuffed arms against the truck.

Bubba looked down at the man's boot-covered feet.

Steel-toed boots, unless he missed his guess.

Glancing back toward the cruiser, he noted Anderson and Tara standing outside it, their focus on him and the man. Did she have any idea the man had followed her from the hospital?

He shone the light directly in Mr. Dubois's face. Although he couldn't smell any alcohol, the man did have priors. "Sir, I'm going to administer a sobriety test. Have you been drinking?"

"Only a couple of beers back home."

"How long ago?" Bubba checked the man's pupils.

"Several hours."

"How many beers is a couple?" Bubba pulled a pencil from his pocket and held it about a foot from the man's nose, keeping it slightly above eye level.

"Just two."

"Uh-huh. Okay, you know the drill. Don't move your head, but follow the pencil with your eyes." He slowly moved the pencil forty-five degrees to the right, back to center, then to the left before center again.

The man's tracking wasn't smooth, which was obvious at

the forty-five-degree angle. Nystagmus. He was over the legal limit.

He replaced the pencil and cleared his throat. "Mr. Dubois, you're under arrest for driving under the influence."

"I'm not drunk. Look, I had two beers hours ago." His head slumped. "I can't get another DUI or they'll revoke my license and my insurance will cancel me."

"Why were you following Ms. LeBlanc?"

"I wasn't fol—"

Bubba grabbed the man's upper arm. "Come on, let's get you to the station."

Mr. Dubois stiffened. "Wait. I'll tell ya."

Bubba froze and stared at the man. "Yes?"

"Look, her grandma and that other voodoo woman hoaxed me. Told me they'd cure me of my drinking habit. They lied."

"So you followed her?" Bubba grabbed the man again and led him toward Deputy Anderson's cruiser. "For what purpose?"

"I just wanted to talk to her. See if she could help me."

A likely story. Bubba had heard all the yarns he needed to hear. Nothing new in his line of work. "Sir, we'll take your statement at the station."

TWELVE

The morning sun broke through the dirty windows of the interrogation room of the Lagniappe sheriff's office, banishing the bleakness to the corners.

Bubba nodded for Deputy Anderson to remove the tray with dirty dishes. He studied Melvin Dubois, now sober.

"Now would you like to tell me why you were following Ms. LeBlanc?"

Melvin ducked his head. "I told ya—her grandmother and that other voodoo woman had promised to cure me of my drinkin'. They lied. I only wanted to ask her if *she* could help." He lifted his head and met Bubba's stare. "She's a swamp witch, too, ya know."

Unfortunately he did know.

He tapped his pencil against the notebook. "Why didn't you just approach her, then? Why follow her and ram her car when she was on a dark abandoned road? Sure sounds fishy to me."

"I didn't want nobody to know I was talking to her."

"Didn't seem to bother you that people knew you visited her grandmother and Tanty Shaw."

Melvin ducked his head again. "My wife's gonna leave me cuz of my drinkin'. I just wanted a chance."

"Did she know you'd seen the other two?"

"Yeah. Said she didn't have no problem with anything if it worked."

"So why would it matter if she knew you were going to contact Tara LeBlanc to get help?"

The big man heaved a heavy sigh. "She accused me of quitting with their treatment. Said I'd just been pretending to be working to stay off drinkin'." He shook his head. "Told me if she caught me drinkin' again, she'd be gone. If she knew I'd gone to the little swamp witch for help, she'd know I was drinkin' again."

Warped, but logical, Bubba supposed, to an alcoholic.

The door opened and Deputy Anderson stuck his head in. "Sheriff, can I see ya out here for a minute?"

Perfect timing. Bubba shoved to his feet. "I'll be right back." He followed Anderson into the hall. "This better be important."

"It is." His deputy's face lit up like a child's on Christmas morning as he waved a paper in the air. "The impression of Dubois's boot is an exact match for the one you found on the LeBlanc property. And his prints match the partial taken off the beer bottle you found there."

Yes! Bubba grabbed the report and scanned it quickly. *Thank You, Lord, for giving me this break.*

"How ya wanna work this, Sheriff?"

Bubba smiled. "Oh, let me share this information with Mr. Dubois. I bet we get a full confession." And maybe, just maybe, he'd find out what happened to Marie LeBlanc and Aunt Tanty.

Easing the door open, he motioned for Anderson to follow him in. Melvin Dubois glanced between them as they entered. Bubba loomed over the table. "I just got an interesting report back from the crime lab, Melvin. You'll never guess what's been established."

The man's expression dropped faster than his chin to his chest.

He knew the jig was up—Body Language 101.

"Want to tell me about your trespassing and trashing the LeBlanc property?"

Melvin looked at Bubba's face, but wouldn't meet his eye. "I don't know what you're talking about."

Bubba laughed and sat on the edge of the table. "Are you gonna play dumb now, too?" He waved the report. "Your boot prints were found outside the shed at the LeBlanc place. Your fingerprints match those found at the scene."

"I didn't hurt nobody."

"No one said you did. But you did trespass and vandalize the place."

"She paid me to look for any papers with some dude's name on it, take them if I found them, then trash the place to look like kids done it."

Bubba's adrenaline rushed. "Who?"

Dubois shrugged. "This woman."

Already taut, Bubba's patience threatened to snap. "What woman?"

"I don't know her. She's new around here. Blond hair, a real looker."

Oh, that narrowed it down. "Can you be a bit more specific?"

"Stands about yea-high." He held his hand to mark approximately five and a half feet. "Little waist. Big eyes. And built, if you know what I mean." He gave a leering grin.

Nothing. Getting nowhere fast. "What name was she looking for?"

"Huh?" NASA sure wouldn't be calling Melvin Dubois anytime in the near future.

"The name she wanted you to look for on the papers. What was it?"

"Oh. Wayne."

Bubba tried to be patient. "Wayne what?"

"Uh, Marshall or something like that."

"Ever hear of this Wayne Marshall before?"

"No, sir. Sure hadn't."

Bubba'd get nothing more on that line. "Okay, let's talk about Tanty Shaw."

Dubois wore a puzzled expression. "What about her?"

"You know she's in the hospital in a coma, yes?"

"Yeah, I'd heard that. Too bad. Nice lady." He lowered his voice. "Even if she did lie to me."

"About that, Mr. Dubois…"

"Yeah?"

"Have you gone through her place, looking for papers with the name Wayne Marshall, too?"

"Nope."

"Why not? You'd go through one voodoo lady's stuff but not another?"

"That lady didn't tell me to look at Tanty Shaw's. So why would I if I wasn't told to?"

The man had a point. A very valid point.

"Thank you, Mr. Dubois." Bubba got up and headed for the door.

"What about *me,* Sheriff?"

"What *about* you?"

"Since I helped ya out and all, aren't ya gonna release me?"

"I don't think so, Mr. Dubois. You'll still have the DUI charge, as well as the trespassing and vandalizing." He left the room, nodding at Anderson as he did.

He couldn't wait to tell Tara they'd found the man who trashed her place. Wait a minute. If he spent more time with her, he'd want to hold her, comfort her again.

His stomach tightened as he drove to the hospital. He'd visit with Aunt Tanty, then catch Tara before her visitation. Maybe that would limit the time he actually had to spend in her presence.

He parked his truck and strode into the hospital. Checking his watch in the elevator, Bubba estimated he'd have approximately twenty minutes with Aunt Tanty before he'd have to lurk in the halls, waiting for Tara to show. Maybe there'd be a change with Aunt Tanty.

Please, Lord, touch her with Your healing hand.

The ICU floor was cooler than the other areas of the hospital. Bubba shivered as he headed down the hall. Two of the nurses at the station nodded as he passed. He screeched to a halt at the open doorway of Aunt Tanty's room.

Tara sat on the edge of the bed, gently stroking Aunt Tanty's still hand.

Bubba's heart twisted. He watched as she leaned closer to the lifeless form and spoke quietly, rhythmically.

He stepped back quickly as Tara glanced over her shoulder toward the door. His heartbeat echoed in his head. This was stupid. He was a grown man, a lawman, and he ducked for cover from a woman?

He gritted his teeth. No way!

Tara spoke the incantation with respect as she slipped the dropper back into the vial. Two more drops of the healing potion, and Tanty could be on her way to waking up. Excitement made Tara's flesh tingle.

"What do you think you're doing?"

Tara jumped and clutched the vial. She spun and faced the doorway.

And a very angry Bubba Theriot.

His face became ruddy and his eyes widened. But the tips of his ears, which had turned fire-engine red, were the purest indication of his anger. She could almost see the smoke puffing out.

He crossed the room, his mere presence filling the small space. "I asked, what are you doing?" He took her hand and pried the vial from her clasp. "What's this?"

"A h-healing potion." Her pulse pounded in her ears.

"You've got to be kidding me." No trace of amusement flickered in his eyes.

"It worked for Grandmere."

He narrowed his eyes. "You gave this stuff to your grand-mother, too?"

She nodded. "And Grandmere came out of the coma after I gave her the second dose."

The muscles in his jaw jumped.

"I'm certain it works, Sheriff."

"What's in it?" He shook the vial.

"Herbs. Leaves. All natural stuff."

"Did it ever occur to you that this stuff could be what's making your grandmother sick now?"

The air rushed from her lungs. No, it couldn't be. A healing potion had never made anyone sick. Ever.

"You could be poisoning them."

"It's not poison. It's all straight from the earth. Not an ar-tificial substance in it."

"There are a lot of things from nature that can make you sick—certain mushrooms, toxic plants and berries...."

But she knew what she was doing. She knew the proper

ingredients and how to mix them and boil them at just the right temperature to remove any toxins.

Didn't she?

Oh, no. What if she'd messed something up? What if she'd been off by just a degree or so and she *was* responsible for Grandmere's severe pain?

He palmed the vial. "I'm going to have the lab run tests on this." He pointed at her, eyes glaring. "You go sit in the waiting room until I get back. Do. Not. Leave. And that's an order."

She swallowed and nodded, then slunk from the room. *Could* she have made a miscalculation somewhere? She shook her head as she entered the waiting room. No, she'd checked and double-checked the recipe. She'd followed it to the nth degree.

But she *had* been distracted when grinding and during the initial preparation.

She groaned. How many times had both Grandmere and Tanty warned her to keep focused when preparing her potion ingredients? It was entirely possible she was to blame for Grandmere's pain and Tanty's not being healed.

Dropping her head into her hands, she rocked herself.

A hand on her shoulder brought her up short. Even more when she met the gaze of Suzie Richard.

"Are you okay?"

Tara swallowed. "Uh…yeah."

"You don't look so good. Has something happened with your grandmother?"

Aside from her maybe being responsible for causing the pain? "I haven't seen her yet this morning."

"Your sister updated us earlier." Suzie waved toward the group of women huddled in a corner, Bibles open on laps. "She said the doctor was still keeping Marie on heavy doses of pain medication, but her vitals were stable and strong."

Great. The pain was still there. All her fault.

Suzie squeezed her shoulder. "We're praying for her—and for you."

For some reason she couldn't fathom, Tara wanted to cry. Sob. Let someone hold her like the sheriff had and tell her everything would be okay.

Suzie's expression was so kind. All the women in Godly Women had been more than considerate, actually. They'd been up at the hospital around the clock, keeping a prayer vigil not only for Grandmere, but for Tanty, as well. Bringing up coffee and pastries to share with the family. They'd been a big comfort to CoCo and Alyssa with their soft prayers and gentle demeanors. Peaceful, that's the word she'd use to describe them. And she was anything but at the moment. It made her want to cry out.

No, she couldn't break down here. She refused. Not now. She still had to face the sheriff. Tara's gut tightened, nausea threatening to overtake the guilt.

"It's going to be okay, Tara."

She blinked back the tears. "Suzie, I'm sorry I was so callous with you. But you understand why I had to question you, don't you?"

Moisture pooled in Suzie's eyes and she dropped to the chair beside Tara. "I do. But I assure you, I had nothing to do with either lady's illness. You'll have to trust me."

Trust. Something that didn't come easily to her. Tara sighed. "I don't think you had anything to do with it. Not intentionally."

"But unintentionally?"

Glancing past Suzie into the hall, Tara saw no sign of Bubba. Good. But a nurse walked by at that moment. A blonde. Something about her seemed familiar.

"Tara?"

She shook her head and focused on Suzie again. "Is it possible your husband found out, despite your fear of him doing so, and did something?"

Suzie's hand landed on her stomach. "No. No, that's not possible."

Tara leaned toward Suzie and lowered her voice. "I know you're pregnant."

Mouth agape, Suzie blinked rapidly. "H-h-how do you know?"

"I just do." She patted Suzie's knee. "Is everything okay? Did your visiting Tanty have something to do with the baby?"

Suzie pressed her mouth shut and shook her head.

"You can tell me. I won't tell anyone."

"I...I went to see her beca—"

"May I see you, Ms. LeBlanc?"

Tara jerked her attention to the sheriff. Why did he have to pick *now* to show up? "Can you give me a minute, please?"

Suzie jumped to her feet. "No, it's okay." She looked Tara in the eye. "We're done with our conversation, anyway. I need to get back to the prayer vigil for Tanty and Marie."

Bubba took Tara's elbow and led her into the hall. She snatched free. "You don't have to manhandle me."

"I'd like to shake you right now. Hard." His words ground out from behind clenched teeth.

Oops, his anger hadn't lessened any.

"I should take you into custody."

She flipped her hair over her shoulder. "For what?"

"Interfering with an open case. Obstruction of justice. Attempted poisoning. And that's just for starters." His eyes were mere slits under his brows.

Tara swallowed. "Look, I only tried to help them. And it did work for Grandmere. She came out of the coma."

His expression softened. "Tara, that potion didn't do anything for your grandmother. That healing came from God."

Remorse filled her chest. "And because your aunt's not a Christian, God isn't healing her?"

"No, I'm not saying that. I don't know why Aunt Tanty's still in a coma. But I do know that God's in control." He ran a hand through his hair. "I know well that God performs healing miracles. Look at me."

A knot formed in her throat. "I can understand you wanting to believe in something. I do. But I believe in the healing potion and I believe that's what brought Grandmere out of a coma."

"But at what cost?"

Guilt clamped her lips together.

"The doctors will run toxicology reports on the vial's contents and on both your grandmother and my aunt. If there's even a hint that what you gave them caused their illness or contributed to it in any way, shape or form, I'll charge you. Do you understand?"

Her legs wobbled. She nodded.

"So for the time being, you aren't allowed to visit either woman."

"But she's my grandmother!"

"And you might be poisoning her. I can't take that chance."

Her heartbeat echoed emptily in her chest.

"Matter of fact, I better not even see you at the hospital. Period. Got that?"

Tears threatened to burst. She nodded.

"And don't leave town."

She cleared her throat. "I understand. Are we done now?"

He stared at her a long moment, something unrecognizable

filling his eyes. Then he sighed. She wondered if he wanted to shake her or hug her. Maybe both. Then his gaze hardened. "Yes. You can leave."

She turned and walked to the elevator. Her first impulse was to get mad—how dare he treat her like a criminal? She punched the button for the first floor hard.

But if he was right, she *was* a criminal. One of the worst kinds. One of those who hurt the ones closest to them.

If that was true, how could she ever live with herself?

THIRTEEN

Now what? Bubba stared at the LeBlanc home, his emotions playing havoc with his logic. The morning sun shone brightly over the bayou, promising nothing but blue skies and high temperatures. The town would crack apart if rain didn't come soon. What was he thinking? The town was already cracking up.

The toxicology reports had come back on Mrs. LeBlanc and Aunt Tanty, as well as on the contents of the vial. While Tara's "potion" wouldn't cause a coma, it could cause severe stomach cramping. But the doctors didn't think that was the case with Mrs. LeBlanc.

Aside from all the information he'd gleaned from the lab technicians, he hadn't had time to figure out exactly what he felt for Tara LeBlanc. Part of him wanted to hug her—another wanted to shake her until her teeth rattled. Maybe he should shake her and then see what happened.

He was back to his original question—now what?

Pushing open his truck door, he stepped onto the dusty driveway. She'd done as he instructed so far—staying away from the hospital. For three days, she'd followed his orders. He hated to be so hard-nosed about it, but he had no choice. It was his job.

The wooden stairs creaked as he made his way up to the

veranda. He would do anything to avoid another confrontation with her, but this was also part of his job. He'd best remember that.

Tara pushed open the door just as he lifted his hand to knock. She nearly took his breath away. In denim shorts and a plain white T-shirt, her long hair pulled up in a high ponytail, she was a vision. Face void of makeup, but kissed by the sun.

Whoa! Better stop that line of thinking right there.

"Can I help you, Sheriff?" Apparently she'd lost that humble feeling.

"I got the toxicology reports back."

She drew a sharp breath and moved back, waving him inside. "Have a seat."

"Merci." She perched on the arm of the couch and he sat on the recliner. "There's nothing in your brew that could've caused the coma."

Relief flooded her face, and a twinge of guilt niggled at him. He'd figured she would beat herself up for even *possibly* putting the women at risk, even though she'd intended them no harm. Judging by her expression, he'd bet his annual salary—which didn't amount to a hill of beans—that she'd been doing just what she'd said. Trying to help.

"But?" She crossed her arms over her chest.

"But the mixture can cause severe stomach cramping."

Her face flushed. "Like Grandmere's?"

It'd be cruel to let her think so. "No. The doctors don't think that's what has caused her pain."

She let out a long breath.

"But you can't give them this anymore. Period. Okay?"

"I hear ya."

He shifted. The worn leather creaked in protest. "But they

found something else in their bloodwork when running this last test."

"What?"

"The lab has a new technician who's just out of school. She found traces of the unknown component in Aunt Tanty's and your grandmother's system matching that of the sample we took from the coffee cup."

"That hyde-stuff?"

"Yep." He leaned forward. "And while she couldn't identify it, either, she recalled having seen something similar in a medicine undergoing testing for FDA approval."

"What medicine was that?"

"She couldn't remember. But she's checking."

Tara frowned. "So what does that mean?"

"It means that if it's the same trace delivered in the same synthetic, then we can narrow down who would have access to it."

"Now you sound like you believe me—that someone did this to them."

"With the tox reports back, well, it does look like someone might've been involved."

The smug smile creeping across her face annoyed him. "There's more."

She remained silent and arched an eyebrow.

"The man who followed and hit you?"

"Yeah?"

"His name is Melvin Dubois. Do you know him?"

"No, never met him before he rammed into my car."

"Well, he's the one you saw in the bayou. The one who trashed your place."

The smugness dropped from her face. "Are you sure?"

"His boot matches the impression we took outside your

shed, and his fingerprints match those found on the beer bottle." He shrugged. "Besides that, he confessed."

Tara shot to her feet. "Did he say why?"

What wasn't she telling him? "Do *you* have an idea?" he asked.

She licked her lips, then pressed them together.

"Tara?" He stood, as well.

"I think he was looking for some records. Of Grand-mere's clients."

"What makes you say that?"

"I noticed some of Tanty's client records had been messed with. I figured someone was looking to cover their tracks."

"When did you notice that?"

Pink inched into her cheeks. "Remember, I told you about the unfiled papers in Tanty's workhouse the day I found her unconscious?"

He nodded. Made a connection. "Does the name Wayne Marshall mean anything to you?"

"No. Should it?"

"Mr. Dubois says he was looking for anything with that name on it."

"Why?"

"He was hired to."

She narrowed her eyes. "By whom?"

"A blond woman. New around here. Ring any bells?"

Tara pinched the bridge of her nose. "The nurse."

"Excuse me?" He pulled his notebook and pencil from his shirt pocket.

She opened her eyes and sighed. "I've seen a blond nurse at the hospital a couple of times who looks familiar, but I can't place her."

Oh. Nothing to get excited about. "Probably just one of

the shift nurses you've seen on the ICU floor but never had to talk with."

"No, that's not it. I feel like I should recognize her from someplace else." She bit her bottom lip and tried to think. "I've just been so focused on Grandmere and Tanty. I can't think straight."

"It's okay. You've been under a lot of strain."

"But I *know* I should remember where I've seen her before."

"Can you give me more details about her appearance?" He poised the pencil over a blank sheet of paper.

"Shoulder-length blond hair." She closed her eyes. "At least a couple of inches taller than me. Curvy." She opened her eyes and shook her head. "I can't remember much else because I just glimpse her occasionally. But I know her from somewhere."

Bubba jotted her description in his notebook and then closed it. "It matches the description Mr. Dubois gave me." Finally, a promising lead! He'd get this information to Deputy Anderson immediately. This could be the break they'd been searching for.

"Did he know anything more than the name Wayne Marshall? Any indication why he'd think there'd be something in my shed about him?"

"He said he didn't know."

She flipped her hair over her shoulder. The familiar gesture made Bubba's heart quicken. "Maybe Grandmere will be off the pain medication soon, and we can ask her if she knows who this Wayne is."

"Possibly." He needed to stop staring at her. But needing and being capable were two totally different things, obviously. He also needed to talk to her about their embrace. Heat fanned up the back of his neck. No time like the present.

"Um, Tara…"

"Sheriff, what're you doing here?" CoCo pushed open the screen door and gave him a brief sideways hug. "How's your aunt?"

He cleared his throat and coaxed his gaze from Tara. "Still in a coma, but her vitals are holding strong."

CoCo touched his arm. "We're praying for her daily."

"I appreciate that." He let out a sigh. "Well, guess I'd better get going." He turned toward the door.

"Sheriff?"

The way Tara addressed him now, her soft words almost a caress, sent warmth spiraling through his chest. "Yes?"

"May I visit my grandmother now?"

"Sure. Just no more brews, okay?"

She smiled. "Got ya."

"Brew?" The door had no sooner shut behind the sheriff than CoCo addressed her.

Tara sighed. Great, another lecture. "Let it go." She went into the kitchen and grabbed a soda from the fridge.

"No, *Boo*, you need to let it go. He was referring to the healing potion, yes?"

It'd been too much to hope that CoCo wouldn't follow. "It brought Grandmere out of the coma."

CoCo took her hand. "Oh, *non, ma chère,* that's not what woke her up."

"Let me guess—your God did that." She set the can on the counter.

"He *is* the Great Physician."

Oh, no, not again. She pulled her hand free of her sister's. "Believe what you want, but I know the truth."

"*Boo*, I know the truth. I've been where you are, remember?"

Exactly! "Then how could you turn your back on what's right?"

CoCo shook her head. "It's not right. It's wrong. *I* was wrong. Grandmere was wrong. And I'm praying that one day, you'll realize you're wrong, too."

Fat chance. But speaking of chances... "Hey, do you know a Melvin Dubois?" If he'd been a client of Tanty's, referred by Grandmere, maybe CoCo would remember something. Anything.

Her sister paused, cocking her head. "The name sounds familiar."

"Anything beyond that?"

"Wait a minute. I know his wife, Becky Sue. Nice gal. Goes to my church." CoCo's brow furrowed. "Oh, he has a drinking problem."

"Apparently. He's the one who rammed my car and trashed the workhouse."

"Any particular reason?"

Tara relayed what the sheriff had told her.

CoCo wiped a rag over the counter. "I don't remember him seeing Grandmere, but there were two years between me accepting Christ and getting out of voodoo and her salvation."

Something about the soft edge to her sister's voice tugged at Tara's heart. "You really do believe all that, don't you?"

Setting the rag in the sink, CoCo met her gaze. "What? Salvation? Of course."

"Despite all you were taught?"

"Despite all that."

"Why?" Why was she even asking? She didn't care, did she?

Or did she? All of a sudden, she recognized the peace CoCo seemed to have all the time was similar to that of the women in Godly Women. Could their belief be the source of their inner peace? For the first time, Tara wanted to know.

CoCo took a seat at the table. "In training, we're taught that the spirits come from nature, yes?"

Tara took a seat, too, and nodded.

"Where does nature come from, *Boo*?"

"What?"

CoCo smiled. "If we use nature for potions, and spirits for channeling and chanting, shouldn't we know where nature comes from?"

"The earth."

"But where does that come from?"

"Well, you know there's this theory out there—you might've heard of it—the Big Bang theory."

"We're taught that you can trace trees, foliage, even dirt back to the beginnings of time, right?" CoCo asked.

"Right."

"So if you can trace the elements back to the beginning, shouldn't you also be able to trace back Earth's past?"

"But the theory is—"

CoCo shook her head. "No. No theories. Let's look at it another way. I believe God created the earth like the Bible states. But let's say the Big Bang theory holds weight…" She leaned farther across the table. "C'mon, Tara, you've been taught that if you can't trace something back to its beginning, you shouldn't believe it. So, what was *before* the Big Bang?"

Tara didn't have an answer. Scary. Her heart thudded.

"You don't know, right?"

"It just was."

"That's faith. Not being able to prove. Not being able to tangibly see. But knowing God just is. God is the creator. And if that much is true, then it makes sense that Jesus is true, too. And I know He is because He changed my life."

Enough. Tara couldn't take anymore. She shoved her chair back and stood. "Interesting ideas. Thanks for giving me your insight."

CoCo stood and wrapped an arm around her shoulders. "I love you, Tara. Nothing's more important on this earth than family. Especially now."

Little butterflies burst free in her chest.

First the sheriff hugs her, now her sister turns to total mush on her. To top it off, Tara was now questioning her own training and her abilities.

What was happening to her?

FOURTEEN

If only she could get another dose into Tanty.

It'd worked with Grandmere, at least to wake her up. What else could have? Surely it would work on Tanty, too. She'd be much more careful this time to get her focus just right.

Yes, Bubba had told her not to. And he *was* the sheriff. But then again, what did he know? He didn't even believe in the powers of the potion.

She hadn't *exactly* promised him she wouldn't, had she? Sure, she might be splitting hairs, but she hadn't given him one.

He'd taken the vial, but she had all the fresh ingredients she needed. And she'd be sure to keep her mind pure while she mixed. No distractions.

Tara slipped out the kitchen door and into the work shed. CoCo and Alyssa were in the living room watching television with their husbands after supper. They wouldn't emerge again for hours. CoCo had given Tara her visiting time, so she had almost two hours to mix the potion. Plenty of time.

The shed trapped humidity inside. Tara shoved windows open and propped the door open. Then she gathered the ingredients and lit the burner.

Tree frogs sang along the bayou. The distinct smells of fresh soil and bayou drifted inside, wrapping around Tara as she worked. Once all the ingredients were blended, she set the flask on the burner and stepped back.

Her thoughts and heart had remained focused during the entire process. Nothing would cause the potion to bring on any side effects. Not this time. She'd made sure.

CoCo's soft words skipped across her mind. The questions she'd posed. The implications she'd made in her quiet and nonthreatening manner. Could CoCo be on to something?

No! Tara wouldn't consider such a thing. They were wrong. She was right. She knew it.

A bubble drifted to the top of the flask and soon the potion was boiling. Done. Tara filled a new vial, then went about cleaning her workstation.

In the distance, the hum of an engine carried over the still bayou. Tara clutched the rag she held, listening.

The engine noise grew closer. Someone had turned into the canal off the main bayou shoot.

Tara slipped the vial into her pocket, turned off the lights, went out and shut the door behind her. She made fast tracks down to the bayou's edge, ducking behind bushes and trees as she did. While the sheriff might've arrested Melvin Dubois for trashing her place, someone else was now close to her property and whoever it was didn't belong there.

Before the boat reached a point where Tara could make it out clearly, it maneuvered to the other side of the bayou, its engine idling. Tara raced to the edge of the bayou. As soon as she broke free of the tree line, the boat revved to life, whirring and gunning toward the open waterway.

Squinting, she could make out the last three call letters from the running lights—U G S. They hadn't done anything illegal, so she couldn't file a report. But just their presence there, at night, was suspect. She'd remember those letters, just in case.

She stuck her head into the living room just long enough to let her family know she was on her way to the hospital, then raced to her Mustang. With a little luck, she'd slip in and give Tanty a last dose of the potion, then still make her visiting time with Grandmere.

A breeze whispered across the parking lot as Tara hurried to the hospital entrance and went in. Heat lightning flashed across the sky, teasing and tormenting with no promise of rain.

She took the elevator to the fourth floor and made it past the first turn toward Tanty's room when a nurse stopped her.

"Ms. LeBlanc, we were just about to call your family."

Tara's heart missed a beat. "What's wrong with my grandmother?"

The nurse smiled. "Oh, nothing's wrong, honey. Her pain has diminished greatly, and the doctor has ordered her medication decreased. She should be awake and alert in the morning."

Feeling as if her knees would give, Tara balanced herself against the wall. "That's wonderful news."

"Yeah, honey, it is. I'm sure you can't wait to see her and tell your sisters."

"Yes, ma'am. I'll be visiting her shortly." Tara straightened and moved to proceed down the hall. *"Merci."*

"Bienvenue."

Tara left the nurse and snuck inside Tanty's room. No one had seen her. Tanty's color looked better, at least to Tara. She sat gently on the edge of the bed. "I've got the healing potion for you."

Unscrewing the top, Tara pulled potion into the dropper.

With a steady hand, she eased the dropper into Tanty's mouth and administered four drops. She leaned forward and closed her eyes.

A strong hand wrapped around hers and the vial. "What're you doing?"

Her eyes shot open.

Sheriff Theriot held her hand tight in his grip. "I thought we agreed no more of this."

She hopped to her feet. "No, you said not to. I just said I understood."

His face turned an interesting shade of red. "Tara, you've given me no choice." He pried the vial from her hand.

"It can help her."

"I told you not to, and you totally ignored my directive."

"But you don't understand. This potion ca—"

He grabbed her by the arm and led her to the door. "I can't trust you."

Her heart did a somersault. His statement hurt more than anything. "Look, I'm trained to do this. Trained by the very woman I'm trying to help."

"And I've told you not to. You blatantly disregarded my order. Not only as sheriff, but as Tanty's closest living relative."

Fear made her heart pump faster.

"I have no choice but to take you in."

Take her in? Was he insane? "You can't be serious."

"I'm dead serious." And by his expression and the hardness in his eyes, he wasn't lying.

She'd have to beg to get out of this one. Tara fought to find the right words, the perfect phrasing—

Beeeeep! Beep! Beeeeep!

Tara jumped, as did Bubba. He gently lifted his aunt's hand. "Aunty Tanty?"

The elderly woman's eyelids fluttered, then opened. She blinked several times and turned her head from side to side.

"Shh, Aunt Tanty. It's okay. I'm here." He turned his gaze to Tara. "Go get the doctor."

Tara raced toward the nurses' station. Two nurses were already on their feet.

"It's Tanty Shaw. She's waking up!"

"We're on our way, child," the elderly nurse said, clutching a clipboard to her chest.

The nurses headed to Tanty's room. Tara rested against the counter, panting, her heart pounding. Tanty was awake!

She stared down the hall.

She'd done it. The potion had worked!

"You know the routine, Sheriff. We'll begin taking her off the machines, one at a time, and run tests. Most likely, you'll be able to see her around three this afternoon."

Yeah, he knew the drill. But he wanted to talk to his aunt, hear it straight from her that she was okay. Bubba let out a long sigh. "I understand. *Merci,* Doctor."

"I have to admit, I expected her organs to start shutting down soon. That she came out of the coma on her own is a good sign." The doctor looked at him. "But you know all this. I'll get to work now."

Bubba nodded, his mind racing. Her coming out of a coma was a miracle. He raked a hand over his hair. But would Tara LeBlanc see it that way? Would she give her potion the credit? He stilled. Yeah, she would.

How could he help her see that the miracle was from God and not some silly little brew she'd cooked up?

The nurses were aflutter with good news. Not only had Aunt Tanty come out of a coma, but Mrs. LeBlanc had improved so much that they were decreasing her pain medication. Maybe soon he'd get some answers.

Please, Lord.

"Bubba."

He turned to find Luc Trahan rushing toward him, a huge smile plastered across his face. "Another miracle."

Bubba smiled. "Yes, it is."

Luc clapped his shoulder. "Tara called and told us about your aunt and Grandmere's progress."

"Yeah. Maybe I can get to the bottom of all this soon."

"I'm sure you will." Luc looked at him carefully. "Is there something else wrong?"

Bubba hesitated, then nodded.

"Want to talk about it?"

"Let's go to the waiting room." Bubba led the way and took a seat in the far corner of the deserted room.

"What's up?" Luc sat beside him, his gaze serious.

"It's Tara."

Luc straightened. "What about her?"

"I'd caught her giving Aunt Tanty some of her potion stuff earlier. I told her not to do it again. I thought she'd agreed."

"But?"

"Tonight, just before Aunt Tanty came out of the coma, I caught her doing it again."

Luc let out a heavy sigh. "Oh, man."

"Yeah. So now, I don't know what to do. She's going to think that stuff she brewed is what brought Tanty out of the coma, not God's healing hand."

"That *is* a dilemma."

"How'd you deal with that with CoCo? I mean, back before she became a Christian?"

"Not very well. Remember, we broke up because I couldn't deal with all the voodoo stuff."

Bubba rubbed the back of his neck. "I just don't know what to do."

Luc narrowed his eyes. "She's gotten to you, hasn't she?"

"What?" Bubba shook his head. "Don't be ridiculous."

Luc smiled. "Don't try to deny it, man. Your feelings are all over your face." He waggled his eyebrows. "Does she know?"

"I hope not. I'm not sure, though." He took a deep breath. "I pulled her into a tight embrace the other day. I'm pretty sure she knew it wasn't just a brotherly one."

One of Luc's brows shot up. "Really? How'd that go?"

Heat crept up the back of his neck. "Better than it should have."

"What'd she say?"

"Nothing."

Luc cocked his head. "Nothing?"

"We, uh…" Bubba's tongue tripped. He forced a cough. "We didn't have…haven't had a chance to talk about it."

Luc sat silent for a moment. "You must be asking yourself the same things I did—how can you have feelings for a woman who doesn't love God? I know, I've been there. Not a fun place to be."

"So, I'm back to the question—what do I do?"

"I wish I had an easy answer for you. I don't. Just pray. God's still in the miracle business—today's a prime example. And look how He touched the hearts of CoCo and her grandmother. Who would've ever thought Marie LeBlanc would turn her life over to God?"

Luc had a point, but it didn't make Bubba feel all warm and fuzzy inside. He couldn't imagine Tara admitting she needed anyone, especially Jesus. The idea grieved him deeply.

Compounded with the guilt that he hadn't witnessed to Aunt Tanty as much as he should have over the years, his emotions were as tangled as fishing line caught in a propeller.

"I'll be praying for you." Luc stood and rested a hand on Bubba's shoulder. "With your permission, I'll talk to CoCo, Alyssa and Jackson. We'll all pray diligently."

Too late to keep his feelings to himself. Bubba stood. "I'd appreciate all the prayers I can get. I just don't know what's wrong with me."

Luc grinned again. "Ain't love grand?" He turned and waltzed out of the waiting room.

Love? Bubba shook his head. He wasn't anywhere near that emotion. Sure, he couldn't stop thinking about Tara. The way her eyes danced, her hair smelled, how she talked with her hands. The way his heart contracted when she smiled.

Oh, no. He *was* falling in love with Tara LeBlanc.

Lord, please help me.

Couldn't her voodoo give her a little better direction? Tara stomped through the kitchen, heading straight for the coffee-pot. How had she slept in so late?

Actually sleep had teased and tormented her all night, hovering just out of her reach. It didn't help matters for her dreams to be littered with images of the sheriff. But in her dreams, he wasn't the sheriff, just a very attractive man.

Tara pulled a mug from the cupboard and filled it to the top with the chicory blend. She took a sip. It was just the way she liked it—hot, strong and not weakened with sugar or cream.

She groaned and set the cup on the counter. What had happened to her? Amidst all the hoopla at the hospital last night with Tanty waking and Grandmere making such a vast improvement, Bubba hadn't been able to finish scolding her about the healing potion. Or arrest her, for that matter. He'd never accept the truth that voodoo worked, just as she couldn't believe in his—and her sisters' and Grandmere's—Jesus.

They were worlds apart, yet every time she'd seen him since Grandmere had awakened, his gaze did something to her. Something strange. Her heart would do little flips. Butterflies would flutter in her stomach. Her arms would feel tingly. What was she going to do?

The phone rang, pulling Tara from her thoughts. She moved to get the phone in the living room.

"Hello."

"Tara? It's Jayden."

Why would her boss be calling her before nine in the morning? "Hey. What's up?"

"I hate to bother you since your grandmother's sick and all, but I've tried and tried, yet can't get the books to balance for the last couple of nights. I really need to make a deposit but can't until we reconcile." He paused, then cleared his throat. "I hate to ask, but could you please come by and figure out where I'm messing up?"

"Sure. How about I head that way now? It'd be better for me." And as soon as she was done there, she could head straight to the hospital and see Grandmere.

"That'd be great. Thanks, Tara." Relief filled his voice.

"Non s'inquiéter." If only she had no worries.

She took her coffee and marched up the stairs. She'd grab a quick shower and then be on her way.

Still, her mind raced with all her problems and complications. Her life had become like a hurricane out of season.

FIFTEEN

When Tara stopped in to look at the club's books, she found the problem. A stupid credit card chargeback.

That was what threw the books out of balance. It was a simple issue to fix. Unfortunately one that took three hours to find. Now it was early afternoon and Tara'd have to hurry and get the issue resolved before she could head to the hospital. She'd already missed the noon visitation time.

Tara lifted the offending charge slip in front of her face. Fifty-eight dollars and thirty-three cents. She shook her head and squinted to read the imprinted name.

Winn Pharm.

She didn't know anyone named Winn, unless you counted the member of the Rockefeller family. With a chargeback of less than sixty bucks? Not likely.

Tracking him down would've been much easier had she recognized the name. Now she'd have to search. Tara grabbed the parish phonebook and searched under P. No Pharm listed. Big surprise.

Jayden lumbered into the office and perched on the edge of the desk. "Making any headway?"

She showed him the chargeback. "Know this Winn character?"

"Let me ask Mike if he remembers the clown." He took the paper and went to talk to the bartender.

She pinched the bridge of her nose. If Mike didn't remember, what next? Maybe someone knew who Winn was. She lifted the phone and dialed the number for Luc's sister and husband.

"Hello."

"Hi, Spence. *Ça va?*" The image of the younger man with his shaggy hair danced across her mind. She could just picture him sitting there in jeans and a T-shirt, smiling at the sound of her voice.

"Good. How about you?"

"*Comme ci, comme ça.* How's Felicia?"

"Great." The preacher paused. "We heard about your grandmother and Ms. Shaw. We've been praying."

"*Merci.*" Had she really just thanked him for praying? Sheesh, she was losing her mind. "Listen, I have a question for you."

"Shoot."

"Ever heard of a Winn Pharm, spelled P-h-a-r-m?"

"Hmm. Not that I know of. Why?"

"I'm trying to work on the club's books and I need to get in touch with this Winn guy. I thought maybe he attended your church or something."

"Nope, not one of mine. Have you checked with Luc? He'd know if Winn attended the Lagniappe church."

"Haven't had a chance to ask him."

"Want me to ask Felicia? She attended that church until we got married."

Tara smiled. The couple had only been married a month or so. "Sure."

"Hang on."

After a moment, Felicia came on the line. "Hey, Tara.

Spence said you were needing to know if someone is a member of the Lagniappe congregation, yes?"

She grinned at Felicia's voice. Always upbeat and chipper, no matter what. Felicia Trahan Bertrand was one of the strongest women Tara had ever met, despite her gentle demeanor. "Yeah. A Winn Pharm, spelled P-h-a-r-m. Ever hear of him?"

"Doesn't ring any bells, and I grew up in that church. Are you sure that's the right name?"

"It's what my paperwork shows. But thanks, anyway."

"Come see us."

Tara grinned against the phone. "As soon as I can." She replaced the receiver and chewed her bottom lip. Who was this Winn guy, and why didn't she know him? Lagniappe wasn't that big of a community, and the LeBlancs knew the family names of most everyone in the area. Unless they were new. Or just passing through.

That'd definitely make things hard if Winn had just been passing through.

Jayden returned and tossed the paper back in front of her. "Mike says the only out-of-towner he recalls being in recently is a blond woman. Very sexy—Mike's description, not mine—and the totals could match, but he's not sure."

"So, I'm back to square one."

He glanced at his watch. "It's after noon. Would you like to grab lunch, get a break from this?" Hope flared in his eyes.

Tara chewed her lip again. She'd suspected her boss had a crush on her for a while. While he was handsome and sweet and funny, she didn't see him as anything other than a friend. Not at all the way she saw Bubba, judging by her reaction whenever the sheriff was around. She groaned inwardly.

Jayden stood. "I just thought it'd be nice for you to get away from the paperwork for a bit. Not a date or anything."

"I appreciate the offer, I really do, but I have to finish this up so I can go visit my grandmother." Not a lie, but not exactly the truth, whole truth, and nothing but the truth. It'd have to do for now.

"Well, good luck, sweetie." Jayden winked and bit into the apple he carried. "It's less than a hundred dollars, so if we need to write it off, we can."

"It irks me to do that. Haven't had to do it since I started working here."

"And that's why we love you." Jayden smiled and sauntered out the door.

With a sigh, Tara lifted the receiver. She hated calling the credit-card company, but she had no choice at this point.

She'd figure out who this Winn Pharm was, where to find him, and then she'd collect the fifty-eight dollars and thirty-three cents, plus thirty-five extra bucks for the chargeback.

Nobody slipped one past her. Nobody.

"May I speak with you, Sheriff?"

Bubba glanced at the door. "C'mon in, Suzie." He shoved the bring-a-burger wrapper into the trash. The life of a sheriff meant lousy lunches in the car or office.

The wife of one of his fellow deacons crept in the room and slunk into a chair. Hesitation and worry were etched deeply into her young face. Suzie had to be no more than twenty-five, yet at the moment she had the lines of a woman thirty years her senior.

"What can I do for you?" *Please let this be business.* He couldn't handle dispensing any personal advice. And if it was about Paul, her husband, well, he really wouldn't be able to help. The whole matters-of-the-heart thing was beyond him at the moment.

"I…I didn't know where else to go."

Didn't sound like business. He lifted his pencil and rolled it between his forefinger and thumb.

"I…I'm pregnant."

Bubba's heart missed a beat, then thrummed normally. "Paul mentioned it at church Sunday. Congratulations." He smiled. Paul had been ecstatic.

"*Merci.* But I did something very stupid."

He really didn't want to hear any more, but what choice did he have? Normally when someone said something like that to an officer of the law, the rest wasn't very good. "What?"

She wrung her hands in her lap. "I'd begun to believe Paul was having an…an…that he was cheating on me."

The words *Don't be silly* stung the tip of his tongue, but Bubba choked them back. He didn't know. Sure, he'd like to think a fellow deacon, a friend, would do no such thing, but he couldn't be sure. Who could be sure about another person these days? Especially in his line of work, people continued to shock him.

"Don't look so stricken, Sheriff. I'm not about to ask you to find out for me."

Had he been that transparent?

"He'd just been acting so secretive, not being where he said he was, coming home late without reason, things like that."

Bubba held his breath.

"Then I found out I was pregnant. I didn't know what to do. We'd wanted a family, were ready to start, but with Paul acting so strangely…"

Big tears welled in her eyes. "I thought he was cheating on me. I was scared. Terrified. What if he'd fallen in love with someone else and now I was pregnant? Would he stay with me out of obligation? Would our baby be born into a divorced family? It's all I could think about."

He didn't like where this was headed. Her overexplaining. Her demeanor. The guilt on her face. Was he about to hear a confession of a crime?

"You have to understand, I wasn't thinking clearly."

When was the last time he'd seen Paul? Sunday? Wednesday night?

She sniffled. "I went to see your aunt."

He hadn't been expecting *that*. Bubba dropped the pencil. "What for?"

"To see if she'd help me miscarry." Tears fell from her guilt-ridden eyes. "I didn't know what else to do." Sobs broke her words.

Bubba didn't know what to do, either. What his aunt dabbled in had never hit him so squarely between the eyes. He jerked a tissue out of the box and passed it across the desk to Suzie.

She wiped her face and struggled to bring herself under control. "I don't know what I would've done had she agreed to help me."

"She didn't?" Hope roared into his chest.

Suzie shook her head. "She told me she wouldn't do such a thing, especially not behind the back of the baby's father."

His aunt might be deeply involved with voodoo, but she had scruples. Morals. Relief flooded him.

"She referred me to a doctor, if that's what I wanted to do, but suggested I talk with Paul first, figure out where he and I stood."

Bubba had always known his aunt was one smart cookie.

"I was scared, but I took her advice. I told Paul about the baby and demanded to know if he was seeing someone else."

Bubba felt uncomfortable, nervous, as if he were reading someone's personal diary.

"He laughed at me." Suzie smiled and pressed the tissue to the end of her nose. "He actually laughed. Showed me what he'd been keeping from me."

She dropped her hand to her lap, her smile relaxed and wide. "Plans to build an addition onto our house. He wanted to surprise me."

Bubba finally found his voice. "That's great, Suzie."

"It is." She nodded, but then the happiness slipped from her face and her voice. "He was so excited about becoming a daddy that I didn't tell him about my visit to your aunt."

"Well, I guess no harm, no foul, yes?"

She swallowed and twisted the tissue in her lap. "Actually, I thought that at first. But now I'm not so sure."

"What do you mean?"

"Apparently your aunt keeps records of every person who comes to see her…with a need."

He let that one sit for a moment, trying to grasp the enormity of the situation.

"And now it's possible someone else has seen those records," she went on. "At least, that's what Tara LeBlanc told me." More tears pooled in her eyes. "She asked me about what I came to see your aunt for, and told me it all looked suspicious, but I just can't tell her."

My, my, Tara had sure been the busy little bee. And without saying a word to him.

"She thinks I had something to do with what happened to your aunt. Sheriff, I promise I didn't. I never saw your aunt again after I left her place. I wouldn't." She dabbed her face with the frazzled tissue. "But what if someone else did see the notes and figured out why I'd gone? What if they told

Paul? What would he think of me?" Her body shook as sobs overtook her.

And just when he thought it couldn't get any worse.

She continued. "He'd be so disappointed, or more likely furious that I'd even considered aborting our baby over such a silly misunderstanding." She hung her head. "I'm so ashamed."

Bubba cleared his throat. "Look, I don't think anyone's going to tell Paul. Whoever saw those notes saw them some time ago. What would be the point in waiting so long?"

"But what about Tara LeBlanc? She's determined to get answers to this mysterious illness that caused your aunt's and her grandmother's comas. She'll keep coming and asking questions, poking around. Paul's bound to catch wind of it." Her voice went up in pitch, indicative of panic and oncoming hysteria. Neither of which would benefit an expecting mother.

"Don't worry. I'll talk to Tara, explain that I know you had nothing to do with the comas. I'll get her to back off."

Suzie smiled through her tears. "I'd really appreciate that, Sheriff." She struggled to her feet, and he stood, as well. "And I appreciate your discretion."

Bubba hesitated. "Suzie, you know that keeping a secret of this magnitude from your husband isn't healthy for your marriage."

"I know. I've been praying on how to tell him. Just not now."

He nodded. Who was he to give out marital advice? His own heart had betrayed him—falling for a woman who didn't even believe in Jesus.

Suzie flashed him a smile, nodded and then hastened from his office.

He slumped back into his chair and lifted his pencil again.

First the mayor and his wife, now Suzie Richard. Who else was on Tara LeBlanc's hit list? It was high time for a long talk with her to find out exactly what she knew. Clearly she'd been withholding information from him.

Disappointment and something else, something he wasn't ready to examine just yet, flooded his senses.

He stood and grabbed his radio. No time like the present to clear the air. Get things out in the open.

Father God, please help me out down here.

Not a person's name but a company. Winn Pharmaceuticals.

Tara shook her head. She should've figured it out. It'd been right there in her face all the time. And she'd missed it. Distracted, she'd been too wrapped up in circumstances to see the obvious.

She again scanned the data sheet the credit-card company had faxed over. Winn Pharmaceuticals. Authorized signers were Vincent Marsalis and Hannah Gerard, but as both were on a leave of absence from the company, the card charges had been declined and marked as possibly fraudulent.

Leave of absence, huh? That wasn't what Vincent had told her. He'd said they were gathering samples for research on behalf of their company. The liar.

So everything they'd been doing was a lie. Running about in the middle of the night, taking her foliage, desecrating her bayou. What were they really up to?

She stared at the fax again. The number for Winn Pharmaceuticals' home office was listed. Tara lifted the phone and punched in the 1-800 number.

Time for answers.

SIXTEEN

"She looks amazing, doesn't she?" CoCo's voice vibrated with happiness.

Despite the lack of windows in the ICU, Tara could almost feel the late afternoon sun shining into the hospital room. Tara clutched her grandmother's hand, careful not to squeeze too hard. Since Grandmere was coherent and alert, the doctors had allowed all three granddaughters to visit at once. "She's beautiful." Emotion clogged Tara's throat.

Grandmere smiled. "You girls, *ma 'tite filles,* are the ones who are beautiful."

Even Alyssa had tears shimmering in her eyes. "I'm going to go find the doctor and see when he thinks you'll be moved to a regular room so one of us can stay with you at all times." She pressed her lips to Grandmere's temple, then rushed from the room.

Tara and CoCo locked gazes over the bed and smiled. Alyssa had always been emotionally detached, but the pregnancy hormones must be playing havoc with her.

"When is she due?" Grandmere whispered.

CoCo gasped. "How'd you know she was expecting?"

Their grandmother smiled. "I was in a coma, not dead. Bits and pieces of conversation, I remember."

CoCo smiled. "Right after the first of the year."

"A New Year's baby." Grandmere's eyes glazed with moisture.

"Now, Grandmere, how're you feeling?" Tara caressed her hand.

"*Bien,* considering."

CoCo grinned. "And you look well, considering."

The three laughed, the mix of love and relief almost palpable. Tara hadn't realized how much she missed this—the circle of her family.

Grandmere tightened her hold on Tara's hand. "How's Tanty?"

"Out of a coma. They're running tests, but so far, it looks very good." She grinned. "The doctor said she'll be able to actually eat food for supper."

"Praise God," Grandmere whispered.

Tara ignored the comment and patted her grandmother's hand. "I need to ask, Grandmere—what happened?"

"That can wait," CoCo admonished.

"*Non, ma chère,* it's fine." Grandmere's eyes met Tara's. "You were right, child. I should've listened to your concerns."

Tara eased onto the edge of the bed. "About what?"

"That research team."

Something akin to fear stole Tara's ability to speak.

"What are you talking about?" asked CoCo.

"Tara told me something wasn't right with them. I didn't listen."

"What're you saying?" Tara struggled to keep her voice level, while she wanted to scream with every fiber of her being.

"That young man, the one who rubbed you the wrong way?"

"Vincent. *Oui*, I know who you're talking about." Boy, did she ever. And if she found out he was responsible for hurting her grandmother and Tanty…

"He came by that morning." Grandmere's thin face contorted. "I think it was the morning I got sick."

"Don't worry about the time, Grandmere. Just tell us what happened." CoCo's face had paled.

"We had coffee and some of the cake I'd made the day before." She shook her head. "Was that the day before?"

"*Oui*. You're doing fine." Tara brushed the long silver tresses from her grandmother's cheek. "You had coffee and cake?"

"I cut the cake and he poured the coffee."

"What did he want?" Tara's impatience showed.

"He wanted to ask me about a young man. If I'd ever met him months ago when he'd been visiting down this way."

"Who? What was the man's name?" Tara pressed.

"Slow down," CoCo snapped. "Stop pushing her."

Tara swallowed her comeback before it came out.

"His brother. Wayne Marsalis."

Marsalis, not Marshall. Tara's heart raced, but she forced herself to remain calm. "And did you meet him?"

"*Non*. So he asked me about healing potions."

"What about them?" Tara asked.

"He said he wanted to buy the recipe." She smiled at CoCo. "As if I'd go down that road again."

"What happened?" Tara wanted to know.

Grandmere shook her head. "I told him I wouldn't, and he became quite *fâché*."

Tara let go of Grandmere's hand and clenched her fists. "Angry how?"

"Said he knew that either Tanty or I had given his brother something, and demanded to know what."

"What'd you do?" CoCo asked.

"I told him I thought he'd better go right then."

"Did he?"

"Oui." Grandmere nodded, but her eyes clouded. "He left. I put the dishes in the sink, intending to wash them out, but then I suddenly felt nauseated. I went to the bathroom, and that's the last I remember."

Tara jumped to her feet. "I knew it. I knew something was off with him when I met him, and he almost rammed into CoCo's boat."

CoCo's face twisted into a grimace. "What? When did this happen? You didn't tell me anything about that."

"You were gone. I handled it."

"Calm down, child." Grandmere reached for Tara's hand.

"He did this to you."

"You can't prove that." CoCo shook her head.

Tara snapped her fingers. "The para-stuff."

"What?" Grandmere struggled to sit up.

CoCo adjusted the pillows behind their grandmother. "Shh. Don't worry, Grandmere." She shot her sister a blistering look. "Tara's going to go find the sheriff and fill him in. You don't have to worry about a thing."

Find the sheriff? Not high on her list of things to do. But the scowl on CoCo's face really didn't leave Tara any room for arguing. Maybe now he'd listen to her. Take her seriously. Maybe this was *concrete* enough for him and his badge.

She bent and kissed Grandmere's cheek. "I'll be back. *Je t'aime.*"

"I love you, too. Be careful."

Tara fled from the room, reaching for her cell phone. Rats! It wasn't on her belt. She must've left it in the car after leaving the jazz club.

She slipped into the elevator and tapped her toe as the car descended to the first floor. It jerked to a stop, highlighted by the electronic ding. The doors seemed to take forever to slide open.

Tara stepped from the car and turned toward the front door. From the corner of her eye, she caught a glimpse of the blond nurse in the elevator across from her.

The nurse's eyes widened in recognition.

So did Tara's. She moved toward the elevator, only to have the doors close in her face.

That woman wasn't a nurse. She was the blond with Winn Pharmaceuticals—Hannah. The one who'd been with Vincent on the boat and in the bayou. The one who had signing privileges on the credit card. The one who'd been at the jazz club.

And the one who was posing as a nurse so she could…what? Tara's heart sank. So she could continue to poison Grandmere and Tanty?

Tara jabbed the "up" button repeatedly. The lights above the elevators showed that the cars were in motion between floors. No time.

She ran to the end of the hall and yanked open the door to the stairs. She took them two at a time, pulling herself up with the handrails. Her sweaty palms slipped a couple of times. She wiped them on her shorts as she continued to race up the stairs.

What if Hannah was going up to give them a final dose of poison? One that would kill them?

Not on Tara's watch.

She ran faster. Her thighs burned. She ignored the pain and pushed harder.

Second floor.

Tara made the turn in the stairwell and kept climbing.

What if CoCo had stepped out of Grandmere's room, leaving their grandmother unprotected? What if the doctor had ordered rest for Grandmere?

Third floor.

Eyes stinging as badly as her thighs, Tara continued to race up the stairs. Her heart thudded angrily. Her vision blurred, but she blinked, pushing onward and upward.

Fourth floor.

Tara jerked open the door to the hallway. She glanced at the nurses' station and didn't see Hannah.

Grandmere's room.

She turned and raced down the hall—and once again ran smack into the wall of muscle more commonly known as Sheriff René "Bubba" Theriot.

"Whoa!" Bubba steadied Tara in his arms. He supposed every man dreamed of a woman falling into his arms, but this was a bit over the top. Even for Tara. "Where's the fire?"

"Blond. Not a nurse." Her words came out between pants.

"Calm down. Catch your breath."

"Can't. Gotta…check…Grandmere."

"Your grandmother's fine. I just left her room. CoCo's with her."

Tara finally focused on his eyes. "Are you sure?" Her breath fanned against his neck.

"Yes. I'm positive. Now what about the blond?"

She let out a long breath and stepped out of the circle of his arms.

He felt void. Empty.

No. He had a job to do, and right now, that involved finding out why she'd been running as if the devil himself was on her heels.

She straightened and met his gaze. "Can I just look in on Grandmere first, *s'il vous plaît?*"

Fear and worry circled her eyes. Her sprint must have been prompted by concern for her grandmother. "Sure." He took her elbow and led her down the hall.

She stuck her head inside the room. "Just wanted to let y'all know I found the sheriff. I'm filling him in now." Relief was apparent in her voice. She crossed the room and whispered in CoCo's ear before returning to him.

"Why don't we go to the waiting room and talk?"

"Can we check on Tanty first? Just bear with me, yes?"

As if he had a choice, Bubba thought. He nodded and followed her. She ducked into Tanty's room, her gaze scouring the small area, and then stepped back into the hall. "Okay. Let's just talk out here, where I can see both doors."

"Tara, what about the blonde? We've checked every blond nurse on this floor and received verification of their credentials from the chief of staff."

She took a deep breath and proceeded to tell him about the pharmaceutical research team not working for their company, credit card chargeback, coffee, the blonde who posed as a nurse and Wayne Marsalis. When she'd finished, she sucked in air and leaned her head against the cold concrete wall.

He remained silent, trying to process everything she'd told him. Nothing made sense, but everything did. He nodded and pushed himself from the wall.

"Where're you going?"

"To talk to the doctors and nurses at the station. Someone has to have seen this Hannah woman. No wonder all the nurses checked out. And then I'm calling Deputy Anderson to stand guard in this hall until we've found her."

The smile she flashed him made his heart quicken.

He ignored his reaction to her and strode to the nurses' station. Work had to come first, even if it seemed all tangled up with his personal life.

At the nurses' station, he requested to see the chief of staff immediately. They directed him to the sixth-floor office.

He made the call to his deputy on his cell phone, then approached Tara. "I'm going to meet with the chief of staff before he leaves for the day and put the hospital security on notice about Hannah. Deputy Anderson's on his way."

She nodded. "I'll wait with Tanty until he arrives. CoCo's with Grandmere."

That she wanted to ensure the safety of his aunt touched him deeply. Too deeply for him to consider at the moment. He cleared his throat. "Do you happen to have the number for the pharmaceutical company?"

"At the club." She snapped her fingers. "Wait. I can get it. Can I borrow your cell?"

He passed her the phone and listened.

"Hey, Mike. Can you connect me with Jayden, please?"

"Thanks." She did a little sidestep before cocking her hip. Bubba smiled at her impatience.

"Hey, Jayden. It's Tara." She smiled as she listened. Her face lit up, and Bubba's heart ached. What was this Jayden to her, and why did talking to him make Tara glow? For the first time in his life, he knew what jealousy felt like. And he didn't relish it.

"Aw, thanks. Listen, could you pull that fax from the credit-card company for me? I need the number of the pharmaceutical's home office." She paused a minute. "Okay."

Again her feet seemed to have a mind of their own. She spun around and made a writing gesture. Bubba pulled out his notebook and pencil and passed them to her.

She shoved the phone between her cheek and shoulder, braced the notebook against the wall and jotted down the number. "Thanks, Jay. I owe you one." A beat passed and then she laughed. Full and throaty. "Yeah, yeah, yeah. We'll see. Bye."

Tara closed the phone and handed it back to Bubba, along with the notebook and pencil. "I already called them earlier and asked whoever was in charge of the credit cards to call me back. My boss, Jayden, said I didn't have any phone messages yet." She glanced at her watch. "It's after four— they might've already left for the day."

Jay. Jayden. Her boss. Bubba remembered meeting him at the hospital when he'd brought Tara coffee. Bubba shoved down the envy at the ease with which she spoke his name. Work. He had to concentrate. "Let's see what I can find out." He dialed the number and asked to speak to the CEO. He gave his sheriff credentials and was put on hold.

"Good luck." She leaned her back against the wall, her palms drumming softly against the starkly painted wall.

"This is Walter Miller, Chief Executive Officer of Winn Pharmaceuticals. How may I help you?"

Bubba told him why he was calling, then ended with a question. "Is the team headed up by Vincent Marsalis and Hannah Gerard authorized by your company to be on a research expedition?"

"No, sir. To be honest, Mr. Marsalis is on an extended leave pending the outcome of a disciplinary investigation. His assistant, Hannah, is on a two-week vacation, as far as I know."

"Disciplinary investigation?"

The CEO let out a heavy breath. "I'm not at total liberty to go into details, but seeing as how you're a policeman and Vincent's in your area…"

Cut to the chase, man. "Yes?"

"We're investigating the possibility that he falsified test results on an experimental drug. The FDA probed and found discrepancies with the results. Vincent headed up that team. Until the FDA and our internal investigators conclude their inquiry, Vincent is on paid leave."

"Thank you for your time and information, Mr. Miller."

Bubba couldn't wait to relay his findings to Tara. Soon, they'd have the puzzle put together. Just a few more hard-to-place pieces.

And then he'd have to deal with his feelings for her, without the excuse of Mrs. LeBlanc and Tanty's case.

SEVENTEEN

Bubba was going to be furious. Even more so than when he caught her giving Tanty more of the healing potion. But Tara couldn't wait for the red tape to be cleared. She needed to move now. And since Deputy Anderson stood guard in the hall, there was no better time than the present.

She headed for the only motel in Lagniappe. The late-afternoon sun hid behind ominous dark billows of cloud. Thunder rumbled in the distance. Could rain be coming? She sniffed the air through the open window of her car. Didn't smell like rain yet, and the sky remained mostly blue.

If Vincent was still in town—and if Hannah was, Vince probably was—then it stood to reason he had to be at the motel. Why hadn't she made the connection earlier? She'd had a bad feeling about him ever since she'd met him. She should've trusted her instincts.

She parked in front of the motel office and strode inside. Anna Grace stood behind the counter. "Hey, Tara. Whatcha doing around here? Need a room?" She raised her penciled-on eyebrows and sneered. "For an hour?"

She so didn't have the time or energy to deal with Anna Grace. The girl had been bitter toward all the LeBlancs ever since CoCo married Luc. Poor thing, thinking Luc could ever be interested in her.

"I need to know if you have a Vincent Marsalis registered here." Tara leaned one elbow on the counter, her gaze flicking to the registration book.

Anna Grace pulled the book toward her. "Now, Tara, I can't give out such information. We're a discreet business."

She'd better think fast before Anna Grace kicked her out, or worse, called the sheriff. Tara flashed a plastic smile and leaned closer to Anna Grace. She lowered her voice to a conspirator's tone. "Actually I was supposed to meet him later, but I forgot his room number." She winked. "Help a sistah out, Anna Grace. I don't want to have to call him and tell him I forgot. Whatever would he think?" She batted her lashes and let her smile creep wider.

Anna Grace cocked her head. "You sure? Cuz I thought he had that woman with him."

"Hannah?" Tara gave a fake chuckle. "She just *wishes* he was with her, if you know what I mean."

"Well, they did book separate rooms. If they were together-together, they'd have shared a room, yes?"

"Yeah. But they didn't." Tara glanced over her shoulder, as if she didn't want to be overheard. Like there was anybody else was in the motel lobby, or anybody would care. "Thing is, he's been trying to get away from her. The woman's a bit delusional." She shook her head. "Always dressing up in scrubs like a nurse and wanting him to play doctor."

"How sad. But you know, I've seen her coming and going in those scrubs."

Good, she'd just gotten confirmation. She'd have to remember to tell Bubba. Then she swallowed, remembering he was most likely having a fit about now, knowing she'd left and not knowing where she'd gone. She refocused on Anna Grace. "Yeah, it is sad. So, anyway, can you help me out?"

Anna Grace chewed her bottom lip. "I'm not supposed to."

"I'm not asking you to give me a key or anything." She fixed her expression in what she hoped came across as pathetic. "I don't want him to think I don't care enough to remember the number."

"Okay. Just this once." Anna Grace turned the registration book to face Tara and let her finger fall on Vincent's signature.

Room eight. Tara smiled at Anna Grace and turned the book back around. "*Merci.* I really appreciate it."

"Yeah. But he's not in the room."

"Do you know where he is?"

"Well, he normally hangs out at the jazz club in the evening. At least, that's what I've heard."

"Really?" Tara considered her options. Maybe Vincent would be more inclined to talk to her, let something slip, if he was in a place he felt comfortable. Less likely to be on the defense. And she hadn't exactly been very hospitable the couple of times she'd met him.

"He even invited me to join him one night after closing." Anna Grace wore a sly smile.

"*Merci.*" Tara left the motel office without another word. She slammed her Mustang into gear, heading toward the jazz club.

"She did what?" Bubba glared at his deputy.

"Said she had someplace to go as soon as I got here." Gary Anderson looked like a scolded child.

She was supposed to have stayed put and waited for him. Bubba bit back the retort he'd already formed. It wasn't his deputy's fault Tara had gone AWOL. "Did she happen to ask you to tell me anything?"

Anderson shook his head. "No, sir."

"Okay." Bubba let out a long breath, hoping to release some frustration along with the air. Didn't work. "I'll check in Mrs. LeBlanc's room. You stay put. No one but Dr. Wahl, Nurse Denham and Nurse Norris are allowed inside. Got that?"

"Yes, sir."

"I have my cell on if you need me." Bubba made quick steps to Marie LeBlanc's room. He inched open the door to find CoCo and Luc sitting with her.

"Hello, Sheriff."

"Evening, Mrs. LeBlanc. How're you feeling?"

"Bien."

Luc was on his feet and met him at the door. "What's wrong? You look like your hunting dog just broke his leg. Is it your aunt?"

"No. It's your sister-in-law."

"What's Tara done now?"

"She's missing."

"Missing?" Luc lowered his voice even as he glanced over his shoulder at his wife.

"Yeah. I left her with Aunt Tanty while I met with the chief of staff. I get back to find she's gone."

"No explanation?"

"She didn't tell my deputy a thing except she had some-place to go."

Luc rubbed his chin. "Any clue?"

Bubba shook his head. "No. You got any ideas?"

"Nope. Maybe CoCo will think of something."

"I don't want to worry her if it's just Tara being, well, Tara."

Luc shot him a sly smile. "Still under your skin, is she?"

"I can't worry about that now." Nor could he tamp down the worry that Tara was doing something stupid and dangerous.

"Then we *should* tell CoCo."

"What're you boys whispering about so secretlike?" Mrs. LeBlanc asked.

Luc went and planted a kiss on her hand. "Aren't men supposed to keep secrets about manly things?"

The older woman laughed.

Luc glanced at his wife. "Honey, the sheriff needs to ask you a few questions. Why don't y'all go down to the waiting room? I'll stay here and flirt with your grandmother."

Mrs. LeBlanc laughed again.

CoCo wasn't fooled. She smiled at her grandmother, but narrowed her eyes as she passed Bubba and went out to the hall. The door had barely closed when she lit into him. "What's going on?"

"Your sister. Tara. She's missing."

"Missing how?"

He explained the situation, then waited.

"Have you tried her cell?"

"Twice. It went straight to voice mail."

"Then she's rejecting your calls."

Was that supposed to make him feel better? "Do you have any idea where she might've gone?"

"Have you tried at home?"

"Jacks said she hasn't been there since she left this morning. He and Alyssa are getting ready to head up here as soon as Alyssa eats all her crackers."

CoCo gave a small smile. "Morning sickness seems to hit Al more in the evening." She ran a finger along her bottom lip. "Have you checked at the jazz club? She might've gone there to finish up the paperwork on that chargeback."

"I didn't even think of that."

"If she's not there, then I don't know where she could be. Want me to try and call her cell? Maybe she'll answer my call."

"Let me check at the club first. I don't want her to jump down my throat for calling her sisters on her. Not again."

CoCo cocked a brow and narrowed her eyes. "Is there something going on between you two that I should know about?"

Heat flooded his face. "I, uh, I…"

She laughed. "Oh, my. You've got it bad, don't you?"

His ears burned. "I don't know. I haven't exactly had time to consider what I'm thinking or feeling."

"Better keep busy then, Sheriff."

"Huh?"

"If you take the time to analyze your feelings, you might realize you're falling for her. And that would be horrible, yes?"

"No. Of course not."

CoCo smiled slowly, so that the corners of her mouth crept upward. "Don't look now, Sheriff, but sounds like you're protesting a bit too much."

The heat spread across his chest. "Mm."

She laughed and laid a hand on his forearm. "Don't worry about it. You're a good man, Bubba Theriot. Tara couldn't find a better person to get involved with."

"We're not involved."

"Looks to me like you are."

His stomach turned. "CoCo, you know Tara's not a believer. I can't get involved with her."

"And Luc once thought that way about me, but look how God touched my heart."

"Well, it's not that easy."

She chuckled. "With relationships of the heart, it's never easy. And with Tara...well, it's even more complicated."

"Amen to that."

She gave him a little shove. "Go see if she's at the club. And I'd suggest you talk to her about this noninvolvement thing soon."

He nodded and headed to the elevators. CoCo was right. He needed to figure out what this thing with Tara was.

But first he had to find her.

He gunned his truck in the direction of the jazz club. His cell phone rang. He whipped into the first driveway he came to and answered the phone. "Sheriff Theriot."

"Sheriff, it's Missy."

The dispatcher. If this was something that could've waited, he'd be annoyed. Time was wasting, and he was parked—he glanced around—at the Lagniappe diner. "Go ahead, Missy."

"You got a call from a lab technician."

"And?"

"Well, she said she'd tried to call your cell, but the call wouldn't go through."

Probably when he was in the chief of staff's office. Sometimes the higher floors of the hospital caused lousy reception. "What'd she say?"

"Said to tell you that she remembered the company doing studies on the drug you and she had discussed."

The one with the paraldehyde component. "Yeah?"

"Yeah. Said it was Winn Pharmaceutical. Does that make sense?"

In more ways than one. "Thanks, Missy." He closed the

phone before she could respond and rested his chin on the steering wheel.

Vincent Marsalis had to be the one responsible. Every bit of evidence pointed directly to him. Now it was up to Bubba to prove it.

To get justice for Aunt Tanty and Mrs. LeBlanc. To make it up to Tara for not believing her in the first place.

EIGHTEEN

The bass thumped, and the treble made the glass candleholders on the tables vibrate. The volume in the jazz club could register an eight on the Richter scale.

Despite that, Tara spotted Vincent as she wove through the throng of dancers to the bar. Cigarette smoke mixed with the random cigar hovered in the air. Add in about twenty different brands of perfume and cologne and the room stank.

Tara sidled up to Vincent and smiled wide.

He smiled back, recognized her, then frowned. "Well, well, well, if it isn't the guardian of the bayou. Come to run me out of town?"

Butterflies tore into her stomach. She offered a shaky smile. "I don't blame you. I haven't been exactly hospitable to you, have I?"

"Hardly." He glared at her.

"Look, I think we got off on the wrong foot. I'm sorry for snapping at you. It's just that I've been under a lot of strain, what with my grandmother being in the hospital and all."

"I heard about that. Sorry."

Yeah, she just bet he was. The creep—he was to blame!

No, she couldn't let her disgust show. "So I've been a bit snappy lately, and I'm just real particular about the bayou. And my property."

"Yeah, I can see that."

"So, what do you say?" She offered a trembling hand. "Truce? Can we start over?"

He eyed her hand before taking her palm and shaking. "Sure. Let me buy you a drink."

"I'd like that." She smiled and knocked on the bar. "Mike?"

The bartender glanced at Tara, then Vincent, and then back at Tara. "Can I get you something?" His look clearly said he didn't approve of her choice of companionship. Was he aware of Jayden's crush on her? She'd have to explain later.

"Soft drink, *merci*."

Vincent gave her a hard stare. "Just a cola? Are you kidding me?"

She swallowed, recognizing the distrust leaping back into his eyes. "I'm taking medication that can't be mixed with alcohol."

"Oh." He barely glanced at Mike. "I'll have another whiskey sour."

Mike stared at Tara. "Want me to bring them to the table?"

She smiled her relief. "Yes, *merci*." She pushed off the bar and led Vincent toward the table in the back corner, the one Jayden kept reserved for any VIPs that might show up. Not that Lagniappe ever had real VIPs, but occasionally a political figure would drop by and it made them feel important to have a table held.

Tara slipped into the booth, expecting Vincent to sit across from her. He didn't. He slid in beside her. Close beside her. The smell of liquor on his breath almost made her gag. He was three sheets to the wind. Would that loosen his tongue?

She inched closer to the wall. "So, why don't you tell me about your company?"

"Thought you didn't care." He scooted closer to her, until his thigh pressed hers. The guy gave her the willies.

Shifting, she crossed her legs. "Change my mind." She smiled.

He laid a hand on her knee. "Sounds like a challenge."

Mike appeared with their drinks. She smiled her appreciation and took a sip of the cola.

Vincent stared at her a moment and then downed his drink. He coughed. Tara patted his back. "You okay?"

He let out a violent breath. "That's got quite a bite."

Tara inched away from Vincent. "So you guys are out here doing research? What are you really looking for in the bayou?"

A frown covered his face. Uh-oh, she'd pushed too far too fast. She smiled. "You know, I'm just protective of the bayou because I need the plants for my potions."

His face went slack. "Potions? You do that voodoo stuff, too?"

"Of course. Trained by my grandmother and another lady named Tanty Shaw. I'm good. Real good."

The flicker of recognition was unmistakable. Score one for the good guys.

"Really?" He smiled. "I'll just bet you are."

She let the innuendo slide. "Yeah. So if I was rude, I apologize. I just have to protect what I need."

"The whole voodoo thing is very intriguing to me, I must say." He traced a finger along her shoulder.

"It's fascinating." She squared her shoulders. Didn't flinch.

"So, you make all kinds of potions?"

"Yep. There's a potion for just about every ailment you can imagine."

"Remarkable. You have like a potion-recipe book, or what?"

Vincent's eyes watered. He shook his head and moved close to her again. Laid his hand on her thigh.

The heebie-jeebies snaked down her back. She shot to her feet. "Let's dance."

He followed her to the dance floor. Great, she had to suggest a dance when the song was slow. Where was the fast zydeco when she needed it? Too late to turn back now. She stepped into his arms, but locked her elbows so she maintained her personal space.

As they swayed to the music, her mind drifted. To what it would feel like to be dancing with Sheriff Theriot. Slow. Rhythmic. Comforting.

She stiffened and smiled when Vincent shot her a quizzical look. She had no business thinking about Bubba. Especially not now.

Even though her heart ached at just the thought of him.

And that annoyed her all the more.

Lord, I don't know what I'm doing, so I'd appreciate a little guidance.

Bubba sat in his truck, staring at the entrance to the jazz club. Why would Tara just up and leave without telling him— without saying a word?

If she wasn't in there, he'd call CoCo and have her try Tara's cell.

If she was…well, he might choke her.

What could she be thinking? Didn't she realize how dangerous the situation was? What would possess her to do something so asinine?

When he found her, he was going to give her a lecture she'd not soon forget.

He'd give her an earful for causing him so much trouble. For causing him to worry about her.

For causing him to care so much about her.

What a class-A *cooyon!*

Three drinks later, and Vincent was practically under the table. Except for his hands. They were constantly trying to touch her.

Good thing she moved fast, and his motions were slowed by the alcohol pumping through his veins. And now that he was good and happy drunk, she'd finally get to the truth. And her personal suffering would all be worth it.

"Tell me about your research. It sounds interesting."

"Not as interesting as you." He reached for her, but she stood and brushed imaginary lint from her shorts. "Whatcha doin'?"

"I've got something on my shorts." She brushed again, then sat down on the other side of the booth. "What kind of research?"

He twisted and faced her. "Just looking into some of the plants. Something that might be able to fight cancer."

That was a new one. Last thing she'd expected to come out of his mouth. She didn't even move when he shifted to her side of the booth. "Fight cancer? Whatever would make you think a plant would be able to fight cancer?"

"My brother was here this winter with some friends of his. Kind of a last great hurrah. All his buddies rallying around him to make sure he had a good time." His words slurred, but not with the alcohol. More with emotion. "He has a very aggressive type of prostate cancer. It spread."

"I'm so sorry." And she truly was.

"No, that's the thing. It's in remission now."

"That's wonderful." Was Vincent too drunk to make sense? "But what does that have to do with plants here?"

"Wayne got sick while he was here. Some poison ivy or allergic reaction to something, I don't know." He wrapped an arm around her shoulder and drummed his fingers on her upper arm until the short sleeve of her shirt moved up enough for him to touch her skin.

She tolerated his closeness. Finally she was getting somewhere. "And because he got sick, you think that put his cancer into remission?"

"Nah. He saw somebody here, a witch doctor or something. She gave him a potion and sent him home." He drew her closer to him.

She resisted shuddering, but shifted.

"When he told me, I was furious. He was scheduled to start another round of chemo, and if he'd ingested something that would make him sick, it'd delay his treatment. Wayne was in dire need of chemo and radiation."

She inched farther away.

Vincent followed, keeping his arm around her shoulders. "I ran some tests and discovered his cancer had gone into remission. No explanation. No reason for it. The only thing he had different than before was whatever the witch doctor gave him." He lowered his head and breathed in her ear.

She swallowed the bile burning the back of her throat and turned her head, avoiding his lips. "And so?"

"He's been in remission ever since. No trace of the cancer." He shrugged. "So I figured it had to be something in whatever that woman gave him. I came to find out what that is."

"By taking the plants."

"Hey, I tried to get the recipe off those two old voodoo women. Neither would even think of telling me, and they wouldn't sell it to me, either. I offered them a lot of money."

No, Grandmere and Tanty would never give out the recipe

for any potion. Tradition called for it to be only passed down from grandmother to granddaughter. Tanty had made a huge exception in taking over completing Tara's training. But there'd been extenuating circumstances, to say the least.

Vincent leaned closer to her. "Wanna tell me what's in those potions? I can make it well worth your while. Financially…and in other ways." His lips landed on her neck like a wet slug.

She shoved him away, disgust giving her strength.

"Tara. Who's your friend?"

She looked up to find Jayden hovering at the table's edge. The hurt look on his face made her sorry she was doing this at all.

She stood. "It's not what you think."

"It isn't?" Jayden glared at Vincent. "You're drunk. You're outta here."

Vincent scooted out of the booth, stumbled, but managed to stand by holding on to the edge of the table. "And who are you to tell me I'm gone?"

"The manager, that's who." Jayden tossed Tara a disappointed look. "Did you come with this clown?"

"Clown? I'm no clown, buddy-boy." Vincent reared back a fist and swung.

Jayden ducked and shoved Vincent. "As I said, a clown."

Vincent landed on his back on the table behind him. He staggered to his feet. "I'll show you a clown." He swung again and his fist made contact with Jayden's cheek this time.

Jayden fell to the floor, then Vincent was on top of him. The two men rolled across the floor, fists flying.

"Jay, stop!" Tara tried to grab what she thought was Jayden's arm, but was pushed into a table.

People moved out of the men's way, but gathered around to watch.

Mike, like a sword-fighter from a previous era, jumped into the battle and grabbed both Jayden and Vincent by the scruff of the neck and set them on their feet. He immediately let go of his boss, but kept a hold of Vincent. "There's no fighting in here." He gave Vincent a little shove. "You'd best leave before I call the police."

"Too late, I'm already here."

Tara pivoted and locked stares with Sheriff Theriot. And once again, he looked ready to throttle her.

This time, she deserved it.

NINETEEN

"**W**ould somebody like to tell me what's going on here?" Bubba broadcast the question, but kept his gaze on Tara.

"I just broke up the fight, Sheriff." Mike shrugged. "Can I get back to the bar now? I'm the only one working it tonight."

Bubba nodded, still not looking at anyone but Tara.

She ducked her head, not saying a word.

"Remember me, Jayden Pittman?" Jay held out his hand. "I'm the manager here."

Bubba shook it and again asked the question, "What's going on?"

Tara lifted her head. "It's my fault."

More than likely, he thought, but as a police officer, he had to take reports. "Care to elaborate, Ms. LeBlanc?"

She flipped hair over her shoulder and wet her lips.

"Grrrrrrrrrrrrrrrr."

Bubba caught the man's movement in his peripheral vision. He shoved Tara backward, moving her out of the line of danger. The man rushed forward as he screamed, holding something in his hand. He moved so fast, he struck Jayden before Bubba could go for his firearm.

Jayden screamed and fell to the floor, holding his chest.

The left side of his shirt went red with blood. A piece of glass stuck out of his shirt.

Tara shot to her feet. "It's him, Vincent Marsalis. The one who poisoned Grandmere and Tanty." Her gaze dropped to Pittman. "And now…this."

Unholstering his gun, Bubba spun in the direction the attacker had fled. The front door to the jazz club shut. He yelled for people to get out of his way, but the traffic to the door became congested as women screamed and men filled the aisle. Bubba pushed his way to the door and exited just in time to see an SUV tossing gravel in its wake as it hit the pavement.

He radioed Missy, put out an APB on Marsalis and ordered an ambulance and the only free deputy left on the force, then made his way back inside. He'd find Vincent Marsalis soon enough. Right now, he had to stabilize Jayden until the paramedics arrived.

At the door, he spoke loudly. "Ladies and gentlemen, I have to ask you not to leave the premises. A deputy will be here soon to take your statements. Please be patient, but this is now a crime scene, and you're all witnesses. You may not leave until your statement has been taken."

He found Tara on the floor, kneeling over Jayden. The glass had been removed—a broken beer bottle, now lying on the floor—and Tara pressed her palms against the wound. Blood covered her up to the elbows. Her hands were steady as she rocked and chanted some unfamiliar words.

"What are you doing?" He knelt beside her.

"Shh. I'm stopping the bleeding."

"With what? Words?" He shook his head. "He needs prayer, not chants, and medical attention now. The ambulance is on its way. Move over." He looked for a rag, something, anything to use as pressure against the gaping wound.

Her eyes shot open and she glared at him. "I can stop the bleeding."

"Not like that, you can't." He snatched a tablecloth off the nearest table and folded it into a rectangle that would cover Jayden's wound.

She hadn't moved, just rocked back on her heels and simmered.

He didn't have time for this. A man's life was at stake. The wound was directly over the heart. Bubba shoved Tara's hands aside and placed the folded tablecloth against Jayden's chest. "The ambulance is on the way. Stay with me, Pittman."

"Hurts. Bad. Want. Sleep." The man writhed against the concrete floor.

"Not yet, buddy. Hang on." Bubba looked around the crowd. "I need something to use as a pillow. And grab me another tablecloth to cover him. He's going into shock."

People acted on his command. A wadded-up sweater was passed to him. He ordered Tara to place it under Jayden's head. Someone tossed a tablecloth to the floor. He ordered Tara to cover Jayden's body, while he kept constant pressure on the tablecloth over the wound. "You're gonna be okay. The paramedics will be here in a minute. Just hold on, buddy."

The bartender, Mike, hovered over Bubba's shoulder. "You want me to get people out of the way? I can sit them all in the banquet room until you're ready to take their statements."

"That'd be great. *Merci.*"

Mike barked orders and people moved. Bubba had a fleeting thought that the man would make a good deputy. Soon, the room was clear.

Tara shifted to Jayden's head and laid her blood-soaked hands on his temples. She closed her eyes and rocked, mumbling words.

Enough was enough! Bubba's resolve snapped, as did his control. "Stop it, Tara! You're making things worse."

She stared at him, mouth agape.

"I'm sick of it. Your games, this playing at voodoo, all of it. You're putting people in danger to suit your own purposes. Grow up." He felt moisture against his palms. Blood had soaked the tablecloth. He looked straight at Tara. "Start helping now. Get me another tablecloth."

She continued to stare at him.

"Now, Tara!"

She pushed to her feet and shuffled over to a table, grabbed the cloth and then handed it to him.

He shook his head. "Fold it up like this one. He's losing a lot of blood, and we need to try to slow the bleeding."

Her hands trembled as she complied. Bubba leaned into Jayden's face. "Come on. Just hang on a bit longer."

Sirens wailed in the distance. About time.

Bubba took the folded tablecloth and swapped it for the soaked one. "Hear that? The ambulance will be here in just a second. Hold on."

Jayden's breaths were thready, shallow. His gaze lit on Tara. "I'm s-sorry. I thought h-he was t-taking advantage of you. I didn't know he was your d-date."

Tears welled in her eyes. "No, I'm the one who's sorry. I don't know what I was thinking."

Something twisted in Bubba's gut. "You weren't thinking. Period. Look at this. All of this could've been avoided. But you didn't think about anyone else, did you?"

She jerked as if she'd been slapped.

The door blew open as two paramedics made their way around tables, a stretcher rolling between them. One kneeled down to assess Jayden's condition. "Nasty. What happened?"

"Fight. Got stabbed with a broken beer bottle." Bubba moved out of the paramedics' way, standing close by.

"Shouldn't have removed the glass. It would've slowed the bleed."

Bubba locked stares with Tara, who had stood, as well. "I didn't."

In seconds, Jayden was on the stretcher and wheeled to the waiting ambulance. Bubba and Tara both stood in its wake. A cruiser careered into the lot and skidded to a stop. Gravel dust billowed around them. Lightning flashed, and Bubba could feel the electricity in the air. Lagniappe would finally get some much-needed rain.

The deputy addressed the sheriff. "Ten-eight, sir."

Good thing he was ready for duty. "I need you to take statements from everyone inside the club."

"Yes, sir." The deputy rushed to the door.

"I'm going to the hospital." Her voice trembled as she spoke.

"You need to answer some questions."

She faced him, tears streaming down her face. "Can't it wait? I need to make sure Jayden's okay."

If only she'd stayed out of this. Playing games. Toying with people's emotions.

"Please, Sheriff. Let me go to the hospital now. Once I know Jayden's okay, I'll answer all your questions."

"*If* he's okay." As soon as he saw the fear widen her eyes, he regretted his harsh words and tone. But it was a distinct possibility that Jayden wouldn't be okay. He'd lost a lot of blood and was weak. Tara needed to face reality. She needed to take responsibility for her actions.

"Please."

His heart twisted. "Fine. Give me a second to get my deputy on task first." He stomped into the club, Tara trailing.

Mike met him just inside the door. "I've cleared out part of the office for y'all to take statements privately. I'll keep furnishing coffee for everyone in the banquet room until they're called."

Yeah, the man would make a great deputy. After all this was over, he'd have to talk to him about the possibility. "I appreciate it." He nodded at Tara. "I'll just go check and make sure my deputy's got things under control." He didn't wait for a response, just headed to the office Mike had indicated.

Deputy Tim Marsh had only been on the Lagniappe force a mere six months. Yet he sat behind the desk, asking the correct questions and filling out the proper forms. Bubba nodded at him. "You need me, radio dispatch."

"Ten-four, sir."

Still so green he used codes, instead of words, even in person. Bubba turned and headed back to the main room of the jazz club. He glanced around, no sign of Tara. Maybe she'd gone to the ladies' room. Probably to wash the blood off her hands. He didn't blame her.

He approached the bar, where Mike poured coffee into cups, filling a tray. "I appreciate all you're doing."

"No problem, Sheriff. I'm used to it."

"Really? Do tell."

Mike grinned. "Marine Corps, honorable discharge, at your service."

Ah, that explained his take-charge ability. He looked over his shoulder. "Do you happen to know if Tara's in the ladies' room?"

Mike crinkled his forehead. "Ladies' room? No, she went to the hospital to check on Jayden. Said you told her that was okay."

The sneaky…

"Sheriff, about Tara?"

"Yeah?"

"She's a good girl. Got a good heart."

Yeah, her heart might be good, but she sure lacked the common sense of a goat. And she sure needed spiritual healing.

If Jayden didn't make it, Tara would never forgive herself. She jumped as a jagged bolt of lightning flashed in front of her. She gripped the steering wheel of her car and pushed the accelerator harder. What had she done?

That arrogant sheriff. Blaming her for everything. It wasn't her fault Vincent was crazy. She had no control over his actions.

But she did have control over Vincent and Jayden's altercation. She was the one who sought Vincent out at the club in the first place. And she'd known about Jayden's crush on her and hadn't cleared the air between them.

Her heart ached and tears blurred her vision. Bubba had been right. She was selfish. Determined to do things her way, no matter how many people got hurt. She'd removed the glass because she had the feeling she was supposed to, but the EMT had said it made Jayden worse. This was all her fault.

She pulled into the hospital parking lot with a heavy heart. Where did she go wrong? What was happening to her?

Fat raindrops fell against the car. Thunder rumbled, rattling the windows. Weeks upon weeks of no rain, and tonight it decided to storm? Even nature seemed mad at her.

CoCo's soft admonishment about spirits and nature and God nudged her conscience. Could her sister be right? It sure seemed that she, Alyssa and Grandmere were all full of peace and serenity during the tough times. Could they all be right on target?

That would mean she was wrong. Who she was, everything she'd been, all wrong. The thought sickened her.

Her steps dragged across the asphalt, despite the now battering rain. She was sick of coming to this hospital. Tired of this feeling of helplessness cloaking her all the time. Tired of not knowing what to do anymore. Was it time to change her life?

She addressed the triage nurse in the ER. "Jayden Pittman. He was brought in by ambulance. May I see him?"

The nurse checked her board. "I'm sorry, the doctors are evaluating him now. Someone will update you as soon as possible." She motioned toward the groupings of chairs in the lobby. "Just have a seat and someone will find you when there's news."

Tara thanked the nurse and wandered to the chair area. A middle-aged woman held a coughing child, patting her back with each cough. A man, probably in his early twenties, with an icepack on his bruised hand sat across from the woman and child. People waiting for attention. Tara paced, not able to sit.

She hadn't meant to cause problems. She'd only wanted to help people. Always had. But now…what if she'd harmed more people than she'd helped? Guilt covered her heart like the thick mud of the bayou.

Reaching for her cell phone, she realized she must've left it in the car. She dug in her pocket and found fifty cents. She located the pay phone, dropped in the coins and dialed her home number. She didn't want CoCo to hear about the incident from anyone but herself. CoCo would understand. She wouldn't condone, but she wouldn't yell, either.

And right now, she couldn't take someone yelling at her, judging. Her conscience was doing that enough already.

TWENTY

Father, give me the words. Guide me to do and say what will honor You.

Bubba sat in his truck, staring at the emergency entrance of the hospital through the driving rain, trying to get his heart in line. Night had fallen over the bayou. The rain looked beautiful when highlighted by the security lights.

Lord, she exasperates me in a way I never thought possible. I don't say the right things to her. Help me be a living witness to Your love and mercy.

But somewhere in the middle of all her antics that frustrated him to no end, he was beginning to fall for her. Despite his best efforts not to. He didn't know how it happened, only that she commanded his every waking thought, and haunted his dreams. Her smile lit up his entire world. His heart pounded every time she walked into a room. Her easy laugh and loyalty to family won him over.

Is she the one, God? Am I supposed to feel like I love her, or am I only feeling in the flesh? What was he asking? She wasn't a Christian. A relationship between them would be doomed from the onset.

No response except the pounding of the rain against the truck.

He'd have to trust the Holy Spirit to lead him. Stepping out in faith, he opened the door and ran toward the entrance. Rain soaked him. Thunder clapped while lightning sent jagged spears to the ground. Electricity crackled in the air.

Brushing water droplets from his shoulders, Bubba approached the desk. He flashed his badge at the nurse and inquired about Jayden. The nurse informed him that the doctors were prepping Jayden for surgery to repair a severed artery. He thanked her for the information and then searched the waiting area for Tara. No sign of her.

Where could she have gone? This disappearing act of hers was wearing really thin.

Grace. *Lord, give me grace.*

He lifted his cell. He would check on Deputy Marsh, and then get a status update from Deputy Anderson.

Once he'd completed his job duties, he'd search for Tara. He knew the Lord would help him when he found her.

A chapel?

Tara stepped into the room, waiting for the roof to fall in at her mere presence.

It didn't.

Silence hung in the hospital chapel, but something else lingered, as well. Peace. Love. Comfort. She could feel it in here.

Her footsteps were muffled by the carpet as she made her way down the aisle. She held her breath, sure someone would yell at her, tell her she didn't belong here and order her to leave immediately.

No one did.

She sank onto the front pew, something inside her not letting her bolt out the door. She stared up at the stained-glass wall depicting Jesus holding a child. She'd seen such images before, but for the first time, she really looked at it. Took in the enormity of the portrayal with an open mind and heart.

The face of Jesus held all the peace, love and comfort she'd experienced since entering the chapel. His hands holding the child appeared gentle, yet steady, as if He'd carry the child's burdens, no matter the weight.

Tara found tears streaming down her face. Could peace and love be so easy to claim? Hadn't CoCo told her many times it was a gift, free, with no cost? Only to accept Jesus and love Him?

Her heart surged as the thoughts ran through her mind.

Peace. Love. Comfort.

Could she have it? Was it really hers for the asking? Would He grant it to her, even though she'd denied Him for so long? Could He forgive her for all she'd done? All she'd clung to and represented?

She bowed her head, allowing the sobs to overtake her.

Tara started when someone touched her shoulder. She hadn't heard the chapel door open and now looked into the tearful faces of both CoCo and Alyssa. CoCo nudged her down the pew, and a sister sat on either side of her. Their hands interlocked with hers.

She stared at their hands, hers still stained with Jayden's blood. A stain of her wrong, it repulsed her. But not her sisters. No, they didn't even question the blood on her hands. More tears fell, heartfelt ones. Ones she couldn't even explain.

"Are you okay?" CoCo asked softly.

"I don't know what to say. How to ask." She lifted her face to the stained-glass wall, her heart splitting. "I want to accept Him, but what if He won't have me?"

"Oh, *Boo*. God loves you so much. I've seen how He's been working on your heart." CoCo squeezed her hand.

"He'll never deny you, if you don't deny Him," Alyssa added, her voice hoarse with emotion.

Their words filled Tara's heart with hope. "What do I do?"

CoCo held her hand tightly. "You confess your sins, ask Him to forgive you, accept Jesus as the Son of God, believe He died on the cross for your sins and invite Him into your heart as your Lord and Savior."

Tara took a deep breath, gripped her sisters' hands and bowed her head. Her heart opened, pouring all the regret, sin and condemnation into her prayer. As she spoke the words aloud, she felt the love, peace and comfort cover her.

And the acceptance. Grace extended.

"Bubba."

Her voice was so soft he barely heard her in the ICU hallway. He turned to face Tara.

Her cheeks were tear-streaked, yet almost glowing. She had a look of peace. "Is there any news on Jayden?"

"He's in surgery now to repair a severed artery."

"What's his prognosis?"

"Too early to say."

She nodded. "I suppose you need to take my statement."

"Why'd you disappear from the club?"

"I had to get away. I couldn't face what I'd done."

How did he respond to that?

She blinked and tears seeped out from the corners of her eyes. Without further thought, he drew her into his arms and held her tightly against his chest. Her body shook as she sobbed in his embrace. He ran his hand over her head. Her hair was so soft to the touch. Silky. He clenched his jaw.

Sniffing, she backed out of his hold. Over her head, he could see CoCo and Alyssa watching. Their faces were also tearstained. What had happened? He lifted Tara's chin with his forefinger. "What's wrong? Is it your grandmother?"

"As far as I know, she's fine."

Then, why…?

"Sheriff."

He spun to see Deputy Marsh holding his clipboard. "Sir, I've completed all the statements."

Bubba glanced at Tara. "There's one more you need to take." While he wanted to comfort her now, he knew he wouldn't be able to remain detached. Not when his heart had already been ripped from his chest and laid at her feet.

Tara nodded and stepped forward. "I haven't given my statement yet."

Deputy Marsh, unaware of the emotional undercurrents sizzling between Bubba and Tara, motioned her toward the chairs in the corner. She flashed a parting look at Bubba and then followed the deputy.

Bubba forced his feet to remain planted to the spot, despite the overwhelming urge to rush to her side.

"Everything okay, Sheriff?" CoCo asked quietly.

"Yes." He glanced at her inquiring face. "No. I honestly don't know anymore."

She smiled, as did Alyssa. "We're going to go check on Grandmere. Luc and Jackson are on their way. If you see them, will you let them know?"

"Sure." He watched them slip into the elevator, secretive smiles decorating their faces. What was up with these women? They were all acting touched in the head tonight.

His cell phone rang, snapping him from his wonderings. "Sheriff Theriot."

"Sheriff, it's Missy. Just got a report on that APB you put out on Vincent Marsalis." Would the woman ever learn to use the radio and not his cell phone?

"Yes?"

"We got a report that he was seen at the Lagniappe motel."

"*Merci.* I'm on it." He closed his phone and glanced at Tara sitting calmly with Deputy Marsh. As much as he wanted to stay and talk to her, be with her, clear the air between them, duty called.

He headed to the parking lot in the driving rain, grabbing his radio. He ordered Deputy Anderson to leave his post outside his aunt's door—if Hannah was with Vincent, about to blow town, she wasn't in the hospital posing as a nurse— and meet him at the motel.

Once in his truck, he made fast tracks to the Lagniappe motel. Well, as fast as he could drive in the pouring rain.

Not wanting to give Vincent a heads-up, Bubba didn't activate his police lights or siren. The man had already proved his violent tendencies, so no sense provoking him unnecessarily.

As he sped along, he called Missy. "Connect me to the motel, please."

A twenty-second pause ensued before Anna Grace answered.

"Anna Grace, this is Sheriff Theriot. Is Vincent Marsalis still on property?"

"Yes, sir. But they've about got that SUV packed full. I don't think they'll be here much longer."

"I'm on my way." He should make it just in time to cut Vincent off at the driveway. Which could push a desperate man into doing something drastic. "Anna Grace, right now, I want you to go lock the office door and get yourself into the back room."

"But, Sheriff, what if someone comes in needing a room? It's raining and out-of-towners driving through the area might need to stop and stay over because of the storm. Business has been slow and I don't think my bos—"

"Anna Grace, do as I say. Now." He closed the phone and increased his speed. He grabbed his radio. "Anderson, what's your twenty?"

His radio squealed. "Turning off Main Street now, Sheriff."

Not even a mile behind him. Good, the deputy hadn't wasted any time getting out of the hospital and on his way. Maybe it was time to promote Anderson to chief deputy, after all. He'd have to review the man's file when he had time.

"I'm about to turn into the motel now. Use caution. Suspect is considered armed and dangerous." Well, he didn't know about the armed part, but Vincent Marsalis was definitely dangerous.

"Ten-four, Sheriff."

Bubba whipped his truck into the narrow drive of the motel just as a white SUV barreled straight for him.

Activating his lights, Bubba slammed the truck into park and stepped out. Rain pelted him like little splinters. He drew his weapon and used the driver's door as a shield. No telling what firepower Vincent might have.

He aimed the barrel of the Beretta at the SUV's grill. "Lagniappe Sheriff, Mr. Marsalis. Turn off your vehicle and slowly exit. Keep your hands where I can see them."

The engine slammed into reverse. Tires spun on the soaked pavement.

Bubba shook his head. There wasn't another exit from the motel.

Strobe lights flashed behind him as Deputy Anderson pulled his cruiser alongside his. "What's the status, Sheriff?"

"Mr. Marsalis is trying to find another way out." He shot a grin at his deputy. "There's not another way."

The SUV stopped and sat idling in the middle of the lot. A rapid succession of lightning bolts lit up the entire area.

"Come on, Marsalis. Just get out of the vehicle and make this easy on us all," Bubba whispered.

The engine revved and tires spun as both the gas and brake were held.

"He's going to try to ram his way out," Bubba shouted to Anderson. "Get out of the way."

The brakes released. Tires squealed. The SUV raced toward them, fishtailing and spinning.

Bubba jumped to one side of the road, while Anderson leaped to the other. The SUV hit Bubba's truck head-on and kept pushing. The Ford truck didn't budge. The SUV kept spinning its back wheels.

Bubba picked himself up off the saturated ground, ignored the wetness seeping through his clothes and nodded across the action at Anderson. "Now!" he yelled.

He approached the driver's door, his gun aimed directly at the driver. Anderson did the same on the passenger's side.

"Give it up, Marsalis. Turn off the ignition and step from the vehicle. Keep your hands where I can see them." Bubba kept his firearm pointed directly at Vincent's face.

The man paused, and then the engine died. Both doors opened slowly.

"Don't shoot. We're unarmed," Hannah squealed.

Bubba kept his attention focused on Marsalis. He wouldn't put anything past the man. But Vincent stepped slowly from behind the wheel, his hands in the air.

"Put your palms on the hood and spread your legs."

Vincent complied and Bubba frisked him for any weapons. Finding none, he holstered his gun and handcuffed the man.

"Vincent Marsalis, you're under arrest for assault with a deadly weapon, fleeing police and the attempted murder of Tanty Shaw and Marie LeBlanc. And that's just for starters."

He turned Vincent to face him. "You have the right to remain silent…"

TWENTY-ONE

"Have you seen Tara?" Bubba asked Luc and Jacks, hovering in the ICU hallway.

Luc turned to him first. "She's with her grandmother, CoCo and Alyssa." The smile he wore looked suspiciously secretive like CoCo's and Alyssa's had earlier. What was going on around here?

"I need to talk to her."

"I'd wait a few minutes," Jacks advised, a small smile sneaking onto his face.

Was he missing something? Something everyone else was in on but him? "Why?"

A pregnant pause.

He couldn't stand it any longer. "Will someone please tell me what's going on?"

"They're inside praying," Luc said.

"What?" Tara, with three praying women? Very unlikely. Even though she'd been contrite when she'd sought him out in the ER waiting room, he didn't think she'd go so far as to stand with a group of women praying. Even if they *were* her family.

Luc flashed the cocky grin he reserved for times when he knew something no one else did. "They're praying— *together.*"

Surely he was missing something. "Tara?" The idea was preposterous.

Jacks threw a mock punch at Bubba's shoulder. "CoCo and Alyssa found Tara in the chapel when they got here."

Tara? "In the chapel?" Bubba's knees suddenly felt weak. He'd taken down Vincent Marsalis without a quiver, but this…this took the wind right out of him.

Luc laughed and led him toward the waiting room. "I think you need to sit down and process, man."

"Yeah, pardner, you aren't looking too hot," Jacks added.

Bubba dropped into a chair. "I don't understand." Confusion muddled every coherent thought he could possibly form.

Tara, in a chapel. Praying.

Jacks gripped his shoulder. "Tonight's definitely a night for miracles, my friend."

"Has Tara…?"

"Become saved?" Luc finished. He smiled and nodded. "This very night. In this very hospital."

Jacks squeezed Bubba's shoulder. "Isn't this an answer to prayer?"

"You have no idea how hard CoCo and I've prayed for her." Luc's eyes glistened with moisture. "And you should have seen Mrs. LeBlanc's face when Tara told her." He shook his head. "I thought the woman was gonna hop outta that bed and dance a jig."

Jacks picked up the story. "That woman cried buckets. I was afraid she'd become dehydrated." He chuckled.

"I just can't believe it." Bubba couldn't wrap his mind around the concept.

Tara, a believer.

"Believe it, buddy. And praise God for touching her heart." Luc patted his back.

"Oh, I definitely praise Him. It *is* a miracle. I just don't know what to say." Or to feel or think. This had totally thrown him for a loop.

Luc gave him a friendly nudge. "Don't say anything. Just be thankful our Father gives us miracles every day."

"Amen," Jacks added.

Amen and amen. Bubba's heart quickened and he felt his own eyes fill with grateful tears. Tara, saved.

Could this mean there was a future for them? Had God given him a sign that she *was* the one for him?

Thank You, Father. Thank You!

"To try and get a recipe to cure cancer, he was willing to kill Grandmere and Tanty?" Tara sat on the edge of her grandmother's hospital bed, picking at the edge of the blanket.

The private room accommodated the group, as well as provided a more comfortable atmosphere. No machines beeping and whirring. A window. Pictures on the wall.

"I don't know that he intended to kill them, but he admitted to slipping them both the paraldehyde. Which, incidentally, was the medication under testing that the lab technician mentioned to me. The FDA pulled the testing and is investigating the whole testing process." The sheriff shook his head. "From what I've learned since arresting him, the man was determined to make his mark in the pharmaceutical-research industry."

"Whatever the cost to innocent people?" Tara's heart contracted with the enormity. Had he harmed others in his quest for success?

"Apparently. Winn Pharmaceuticals is now looking into every drug testing Vincent had ever been in charge of."

"What is that drug, the one he gave Grandmere and Tanty, used for? When it's used properly, I mean," CoCo asked.

Bubba glanced at his notes. "Initial research gave the pharmaceutical company hope that it could be altered from its original state to be a short-term anesthesia for simple procedures. It seemed to promise fewer side effects than what's currently on the market."

Tara's head ached as she tried to clarify the jumble of information. "So here are two proven instances when he'd put others at risk. For what?"

"Fame and fortune, of course." Alyssa shifted on Jackson's lap in the corner chair. "Can you imagine being the person responsible for finding the cure for cancer? The glory and recognition?"

The sheriff stared at Tara. "Is there anything in the bayou that could do that? Cure cancer, I mean."

"I don't think so." She let out a soft sigh.

Her grandmother patted her hand. "There's nothing in that bayou that hasn't been tested a million times over during the last couple of decades. If there were such a plant with those properties, research teams would've found it a long time ago."

"That's what I thought." Bubba scribbled something on his papers.

Tara still couldn't understand the logic. It just didn't make sense. "What about Hannah? What was *she* doing?"

"She claims to be in love with Vincent, and believed in his abilities as a research chemist." Bubba set down his clipboard. "She posed as a nurse and injected Mrs. LeBlanc and my aunt with a medication that would cause severe cramping, knowing that the policy in the ICU, if a patient is in that much pain and on the critical list, is to medicate the patient so she's barely coherent. Hannah couldn't risk either of them stating Vincent had tried to buy the potion. She used a drug that is almost undetectable in bloodwork, and that's why the hospital couldn't find any reason for Mrs. LeBlanc here to be in such pain." He shook his head. "The sad part is, she'd planned to obtain more of the paraldehyde to inject in them."

"So she put two women in danger and says her reason for doing so is being in love with someone and wanting to help him?" CoCo shook her head and smoothed Grandmere's hair. "That's insane."

"Partially, but she probably would've gotten some credit if they'd discovered a cure for cancer." The sheriff sighed. "They are both of the philosophy that the ends justify the means."

"Sad." Luc laid a hand on his wife's waist.

"Yeah." Bubba stood. "And that about wraps it all up."

"*Merci* for letting us know, Sheriff," Grandmere said.

He nodded, but didn't leave. Tara's back burned. She looked at him. Her heartbeat skipped.

"May I see you for a moment, Tara?"

She kissed Grandmere's forehead and then followed him from the room. In the hall they stood on opposite sides, silent and staring.

He moved first, holding out his hand. "Walk me out?"

Her heart accelerated as she tucked her hand into his. Warmth spread up her arm and into her chest. She had so much she wanted to tell him, needed to tell him, but the words wouldn't work loose from her knotted emotions.

Once outside the hospital, under the canopy, he motioned toward the stone bench. "Sit with me?"

Not an order or even a suggestion, just a question.

As if she could say no.

She took a seat next to him. The rain drilled against the canopy, steady and rhythmic. The air smelled cleaner, lighter.

As if Lagniappe had also been redeemed. Tara smiled to herself.

"Tara, about Suzie Richard…"

She pressed a finger against his lips. "Shh. Forget it. None of my business. Just like it wasn't my business about the mayor." She dropped her hand into her lap. This doing the right thing was going to take some getting used to. "I just stormed my way through suspects, and I had no right. I'm sorry the mayor chewed you out because of me."

"And Suzie came crying to me in my office."

She felt a sinking sensation. "I'm so sorry."

Would she be apologizing until the cows came home? Surely not. CoCo had promised to give her some information about Christianity when they got home, and Tara vowed to scour the information. Now that she'd accepted Jesus, she wanted to live her life the right way. No more side trips. No more voodoo. And no more spirits—except what she could learn about the Holy Spirit.

"Tara, there's something else we need to talk about."

Here it came, the dissecting of the hug and everything. She wasn't ready to put all her cards on the table about what she'd grown to feel for him, only for him to apologize for embracing her after she'd told him not to touch her. She couldn't take that kind of rejection. Not right now. Her emotions were too raw.

He took her hand and caressed her knuckles with his thumb as he spoke. Little tingles shot all the way to her toes. "I've been trying to figure out how to say this, how to even explain it, and I can't make the pretty words." His eyes clouded with emotion.

Her stomach let the butterflies loose again. Dared she hope?

"What I'm trying to say, rather badly, I might add, is that I have feelings for you. Real feelings. Romantic feelings."

Oh, she was going to cry. Just when she thought her day couldn't get any better, he spoke directly to her heart.

"I know we make each other crazy, but no other woman has ever made me feel the way you do. I can't get you out of my head. Or my heart. And believe me, I've tried."

Tears burned her eyes. Yep, she was gonna turn into a pool of mush, and she didn't even care.

"I'm sorry," he said. "I didn't mean to upset you." He wiped her tears away with the pad of his thumb, his hands cupping her face.

She smiled and sniffed. He was such a *cooyon!* "Oh, you didn't upset me. Can't you tell that I have the same feelings for you? That I was so scared you were about to tell me these feelings—our connection—was a mistake."

He smiled and leaned forward. His lips touched hers softly. She wrapped her arms around his neck and poured every inch of her feelings for him into the kiss.

All too soon, he ended the kiss, but kept cupping her face. "You weren't very good as a voodoo queen if you thought that."

She inhaled sharply. Were people always going to remind her of her past? Then she recognized the teasing in his eyes and laughed. "Kiss me again, or I'll turn you into a toad."

Instead, he swatted her playfully on the arm, stood in one fluid motion and took off running toward his truck. She hesitated a moment and then took off behind him, her feet making splashes on the wet pavement. The rain continued to pour, but it felt good. Cool and refreshing.

Tara caught up to him just as he reached his truck. She wrapped her arms around his waist and drew him to her. He encircled her with his arms and smiled down at her. The rain matted her hair against her face. His gentle fingers pushed the locks away. Standing on tiptoe, she pressed her lips to his.

When he pulled back, he wore a mock frown. "You're going to be a handful, aren't you?"

She smiled. "And you're going to be a by-the-book type all the time, aren't you?"

He dropped a kiss on the tip of her nose. "You're too head-strong for your own good."

"And you're too legalistic for your own good."

He chuckled, his chest rumbling, and she could feel his arms vibrating around her. "Tara LeBlanc, I love you."

Shock held her tongue hostage. She never dreamed she'd be in the arms of the man she now knew she loved, hearing him profess his love for her. New tears spilled from her eyes, mixing with the rain.

"Now, I don't expect you to tell me you love me just because I told *you*. Just whenever you know it's the truth. I'm a patient man. I'll wait."

No, she didn't want to wait. Not for one more minute…not for one more second. Life was too precious to waste. Love was too powerful an emotion to be denied. She should know—she'd been fighting it.

"*Je t'aime*, René Theriot. I love you." She kissed him soundly on the mouth. When she drew away, his expression was one of such shock, she couldn't help but laugh.

Laying a hand on his cheek, she grinned. "Is that evidence concrete enough for you, Sheriff?"

EPILOGUE

What a day to celebrate life and love!

Tara stood at the window, staring down at the side yard next to the bayou. She and Grandmere had ordered the work shed taken down. The grass had already begun to grow where the shed had once stood. White chairs lined the area around the veranda. Soon, she'd head out there and start a new life with the love of her life.

The long blazing-hot summer had finally given way to fall. Over the past several months, the love she shared with Bubba had burst into full bloom. And now, she would be joined with him. Forever.

"You ready?" CoCo asked as she and Alyssa swept into her bedroom.

Tara couldn't help but smile at her sisters. Especially Alyssa, who looked downright precious in her black maternity dress. Of course, she probably wouldn't appreciate the compliment. Tara refrained from giving it.

"I'm so glad you decided to have an autumn wedding. I would've died in the humidity." Alyssa sank onto the bed and let out a big sigh. "I feel like a beached whale. Look like one, too."

"You look beautiful," CoCo said. She winked at Tara.

"And you…you're positively stunning. Bubba is one lucky man."

Heat fanned Tara's cheeks. She turned to the mirror and checked her appearance once more. The dress their mother had worn on her wedding day had been worn by CoCo, and now by her. Her gaze met CoCo's in the mirror. "I wish they were here."

"I know, *Boo*. They are. In our hearts."

Tara smiled. "How's Grandmere?"

Alyssa laughed and pointed out the window to where their grandmother sat beside Tanty on the first row. "Being the belle of the ball, of course. Now all three of her granddaughters are about to be married to—" she wrinkled her pert nose "—handsome, strong men, just like my Marcel."

The sisters chuckled at Alyssa's perfect imitation of their grandmother.

"Spence and Felicia are here." CoCo lifted the veil she herself had worn not even a year ago. "Are you ready?"

Tara nodded. CoCo arranged the veil on the crown of Tara's head, securing it with pins. She stepped back and Tara turned.

Alyssa dabbed her eyes with a handkerchief. "It's the hormones, I tell ya. I never get all worked up at weddings." She gripped the chair in front of her and struggled to stand, her tummy throwing her off balance. "But, Tara, you are a vision. Absolutely gorgeous. CoCo's right—the sheriff's one lucky man."

Tara smiled. "You know, eyebrows are gonna be raised when you two walk me down the aisle."

Alyssa shrugged. "When have we ever cared what anybody thought?"

CoCo and Tara burst into laughter. Alyssa turned red. "Well, okay, so I did. But hey, I got over it."

"It's about what you want," CoCo whispered as she hugged Tara.

"Besides, we're more than ready to give you away," Alyssa teased.

Again, the three sisters laughed together. Tara's heart filled to the brim with happiness. She glanced out the window and saw Pastor Spencer Bertrand standing in the gazebo. Jackson and Luc stood to the right side, looking downright dashing in their black tuxedos with tails. But it was the man standing beside them, in all white, who took her breath away.

The man who would soon promise to love her forever, share his dreams with her and comfort her in their old age.

Tears welled in her eyes.

"Oh, you're gonna mess up your makeup. Stop that." CoCo handed her a tissue and patted her back.

"We'd better get a move on. I think I hear your musical cue." Alyssa cracked open the door.

The opening bars of "I've Been Redeemed" rang out. CoCo turned to Tara and laughed aloud again. "You're kidding me."

"Nope. I think it's fitting, don't you?" Tara smiled. The song *was* fitting. She had been redeemed through Christ, but also in the love of the man of her dreams. "Better than 'I Shot the Sheriff.'"

Alyssa snorted. "It's perfect." She swung the door open all the way. "Now, let's go give you away."

Tara linked arms with her sisters, CoCo on her right and Alyssa on her left. Peace filled her as they made their way to the kitchen door, where she'd begin her walk to become Mrs. René Theriot.

Mrs. René Theriot. It had such a nice ring to it. And they'd be husband and wife.

As concrete as it could get.

Tara smiled. Their marriage might be concrete, but she still planned a few surprises to keep the sheriff on his toes.

Oh, my, yes—she'd find lots of ways to keep him off balance so he'd have to cling to her. And together, they'd cling to God's promises.

Dear Reader,

Thank you for journeying with me through the Louisiana bayou again. South Louisiana is deep within my heart, and I hope, through this series, it's snaked its way into yours, as well.

The characters in this series have become like family to me. It's been fun watching them work through their inner struggles and overcome.

Tara's personality is much like that of my eldest daughter's. Some of the life lessons Tara deals with in this book belong to my Emily. I thank her for giving me permission to share some of her outlooks and insights into this crazy thing called life. She's a wonderful inspiration to me daily, and I hope Tara's story gives you a sense of hope. And love.

I love hearing from readers. Please visit me at: www.robincaroll.com and drop me a line, or write to me at PO Box 242091, Little Rock, AR, 72223. Join my newsletter group...sign my guestbook. I look forward to hearing from you.

Blessings,

Robin Carroll

QUESTIONS FOR DISCUSSION

1. Tara felt like she'd been abandoned by her grandmother. Have you ever felt like someone you loved and respected abandoned you? If so, how did you come to terms with the emotions?

2. Sheriff Bubba Theriot was conflicted between his feelings and his professional responsibilities. Have you ever felt conflicted in such a way? What did/didn't you do?

3. Tara's salvation happened quietly, in a hospital chapel. What is your salvation story?

4. Bubba's personality sometimes clashed with Tara's. Have you ever loved someone, yet had a personality clash? How did you handle those instances?

5. We all want to believe in hope. Vincent believed there was a plant in the bayou that could help cure cancer. He chased this hope in a way that hurt others. Have your hopes ever caused you to harm others?

6. Tara's sister, CoCo, witnessed to her in a nonoffensive way. How do you see *your* testimony?

7. Bubba found himself the focus of the mayor's anger and frustration a couple of times, yet he kept his cool. Have you ever been in a situation where someone took their emotions out on you? How did you react?

8. Pharmaceutical companies work to bring new medications to the sick. Do you believe there should be limitations on their research, based on Scripture? Why/why not?

9. Bubba felt like he'd failed in witnessing to his aunt. Although the outcome isn't written in this book, what do you believe happened later between him and his aunt on the salvation topic?

10. Bubba and Tara had to learn to trust one another in order to find love. How important is trust to you in your personal relationships?

11. Tara finally realized that voodoo was wrong. Have you ever learned that something you were doing was very wrong? How did you handle the issue?

12. Tara was disappointed not to be named godmother by Alyssa. Have you ever suffered from a disappointment? How did you manage?

13. Jayden had a crush on Tara, which she didn't return. Have you ever faced a similar situation? How did you handle it?

14. Suzie Richard almost allowed a misunderstanding to irrevocably damage her family. Have you ever let a misunderstanding overtake your good judgment? How did you get resolution?

15. Tara's family loved her and prayed for her salvation. How might you help someone you know is unsaved?